The Good Shepherd

Skriðuklaustur
ÍSLAND

GUNNAR GUNNARSSON

THE GOOD SHEPHERD

TRANSLATED BY KENNETH C. KAUFMAN
ILLUSTRATED BY MASHA SIMKOVITCH

FOREWORD BY JÓN KALMAN STEFÁNSSON

Bjartur 2016

About this edition

The Good Shepherd (Advent) was first published in Germany and
Denmark in the winter 1936–1937. The first English translation by
Evelyn C. Ramsden came out in London by Jarrolds Publishers in
1939. The English edition that is here reprinted was published by
Bobbs-Merrill Company in New York in 1940. The translation was
made by professor Kenneth C. Kaufman, head of the Department of
Modern Languages of the University of Oklahoma. The illustrations
were made by Masha Simkovitch (aka Marie Simchow Stern). The
book was selected for special distribution by the Book of the Month
Club to all its members as a gift book. Therefore it was printed in
300.000-400.000 copies in the years 1940 and 1941 in the
United States.

The Good Shepherd or *Advent* is the most translated and printed work
by Gunnar Gunnarsson. It is still published in new languages around
the world and read by thousands of people every year. In some homes
it is a tradition to read the book in the weeks before Christmas.

The Good Shepherd
© Stofnun Gunnars Gunnarssonar, 2016
Foreword © Jón Kalman Stefánsson, 2011
Translated by Philip Roughton
Cover: Flash Gordon
Printed in Iceland by Oddi

ISBN: 978-9935-454-91-1
www.bjartur.is

Bjartur | Reykjavík | 2016

Foreword

It appears as if it does not take much in terms of contents to create a masterpiece, a book that is timeless. A man roams the woods with a gun and a dog, mutters a few things about nature, falls in love with a woman, and ends up shooting himself; a middle-aged writer takes a short break from writing, goes to Venice, falls in love with a teenage boy, loses his grip on life and dies; a man wanders the wilderness with a dog and a ram in December, searching for sheep, gets caught in a storm but makes it back to civilization alive.

Here I have described the contents of three books—novellas. This may not look like much, but a book's contents are seldom the most important thing about them; more important, perhaps, is their execution—a simple truth that tends to be forgotten. The three books to which I refer are *Pan* by Knut Hamsun, *Death in Venice* by Thomas Mann, and *Advent (The Good Shepherd)* by Gunnar Gunnarsson.* Little further will be said here about Hamsun and Mann's books, I shall resist the temptation, because at the moment it is

---

*   *Advent* (originally published in 1936) was published in the United States as *The Good Shepherd* (Bobbs-Merrill, 1940).

Gunnar who matters. Gunnar, Benedikt, Leó, and Eitill; it is so good to walk in moonlight amidst mountains. Yet first I must take a short detour before I head into the wilderness, on the heels of this trinity.

There's nothing like a first impression

I may have heard of Gunnar Gunnarsson first when I was in secondary school in Keflavík, but I don't clearly remember having done so, mainly because I've forgotten most things from those years: the knots that I learned in my seamanship course, algebra, etc. I first came into contact with Gunnar's writing when given the chore of wiping things clean at home. Gunnar's collected works, published in the sixties, stood lined up on one shelf, and I made sure not to touch the books with the moist cloth: eight thick volumes with rather small print. That's how I, thirteen years old, met him, in a single-family home in Keflavík. Every week for several years afterward, I stood over his oeuvre, with the exception of his short stories, whenever I wiped off that shelf—yet I never opened a book by Gunnar until we were assigned to read him at university ten years later. It never occurred to me, at least not in any real earnestness, to read anything by Gunnar after I became hooked on literature; we all have our shortcomings, indeed—yet perhaps there are also other explanations.

In the literature of every nation there are certain works, let's call them pinnacles, monoliths, that are so dear to readers that their greatness, and presence, are nearly taken for granted—seemingly escaping any need for critique or even discussion. Gunnar's most renowned books: *The Church on the Mountain* (*Kirken paa bjerget*, 1923–1928), *The Black Cliffs* (*Svartfugl*, 1929), and *Advent*, are such works—pinnacles —yet while not being so, at the same time. We who live here upon the outermost sea have perhaps never truly come to terms with the Nobel Prize that Halldór Laxness was awarded in 1955; since then, there has been an imbalance in our perceptions and discussions of literature. A Nobel Prize can be dangerously big for a small country, our one and only mountain, we say of Halldór Laxness, as if there were just one mountain in all of Iceland, perhaps Herðubreið. No Esja, no Kaldbakur, nor any of the fells: Sauðafell, Reykjafell. Yet those who care, know that the very best in Gunnar Gunnarsson, as well as Þórbergur Þórðarson (1889–1974), of course, stands in every respect on a par with the pinnacles in Halldór Laxness' oeuvre; a simple truth that the Nobel Prize removed from the equation. It's another matter entirely that Halldór displays more faces than these writers, and that his career was more wide-reaching.

No, I never read Gunnar until my early twenties, when I began studying at the University of Iceland. I did, of course, read contemporary authors enthusiastically, yet when I looked over the history of Icelandic literature, I beheld just the one mountain, apart, perhaps, from the peculiar Þórbergur Þórðarson. If my thoughts ever wandered to Gunnar, it would have been in the form of his collected works, eight thick volumes; for me, he existed in an off-putting collection, not in particular books. I know of several other dedicated literati of my generation who hesitated, and still hesitate, in the face of weighty series, uncertain of where to begin, reluctant to be confronted with thousands of pages. Yet there is another factor that complicates matters considerably: Gunnar Gunnarsson wrote most of his works in Danish, not Icelandic. At the age of eighteen, he went to Denmark to study—a farmer's son from Iceland who had in fact published two thin volumes of poetry. He was a writer, and did not want to be anything other than a writer; for him, to live was to write —and vice versa. At the time, however, Iceland was a poor and relatively underdeveloped country; it was part of the Danish kingdom, with Copenhagen as its capital, and it was there that Icelanders had, for centuries, attended university. Gunnar could of course read Danish by the time he went abroad, yet he spoke it little and wrote it even less. He did, however, have a burning ambition: he wanted to make his living by writing, but since that was impossible in Iceland, he left, and managed in the space of just several years to gain a perfect grasp on Danish—so perfect that in the 1920's, he was among the most well-known and popular writers in the Danish language. Gunnar's Icelandic readers are, therefore, now faced with three options: to read his works in Danish, which few people do today; to read them in others' translations, for example, those of Halldór Laxness; or to read them in Gunnar's own translations. In his advanced years, Gunnar began to translate all of his own books; to transform, as an elderly man, what he had written as a youth. Thus, we are now confronted with three editions of his books, which of course also helps to complicate things, or even to hinder access to these books. Most people choose to read the translations, although Gunnar's written Danish is beautiful; yet then there is still the question of which translation to use: his own or another's.

Author of two worlds

Gunnar developed as a writer in an environment radically different to what most Icelandic authors knew. The century's conflicts, the existential angst in the wake of World War I, and world affairs in the 1920's hit closer to home for Gunnar than his contemporaries in Iceland, who perhaps concerned themselves more with tussock-leveling tractors and Danish rule than world affairs. Whether it was because of his place of residence or his disposition—these two, perhaps, being inseparable—Gunnar seemed to have put more thought into the narrative form itself than his colleagues did here in

Iceland; he was more focused, his books better structured, more conscientious. He was, simultaneously, an author of two worlds: an Icelander who wrote in Danish, living in a big city, yet always with the Icelandic countryside as the setting of his books. The city where he lived, Copenhagen, rarely appears in his works, yet when it does, it is quite bulky—as, for instance, in *The Inexperienced Traveler* (*Den uerfarne rejsende*, 1927), the final volume of *The Church on the Mountain*. This work's first two volumes, *Ships in the Sky* (*Skibe på himlen*, 1925) and *The Night and the Dream* (*Natten og drømmen*, 1926) have received praise, while *The Inexperienced Traveler* is considered inferior. This judgment is possibly infected by people's belief that writers, in their autobiographies, put their best energies into describing their childhood years—while what comes afterward lacks a certain gusto. This has been said about Gunnar, as it has also been said of the final volume in Maxim Gorky's magnificent books about his childhood and youthful years, books that undoubtedly influenced Gunnar's writing of *The Church on the Mountain*. These great works of different authors have elements in common, and they both glow with the dark and bright fires lit by the sparks created when reality and fiction are hurled together. I've always had the feeling that *The Inexperienced Traveler* was not given its due; it's our *Hunger*, and if viewed in a broader European context, it could be seen to stand somewhere between Hamsun's work (on the deprivation and starvation brought about by poverty) and

Rilke's "upper-class starvation": the story of Malte Laurids Briggen.

Despite the fact that Gunnar never does, in a certain sense, leave home as a novelist, always choosing a thoroughly Icelandic setting, the fate of the wider world, the confused Europe in the first part of the twentieth century, seems always to exert a pervasive influence on his works. Yet I've sometimes wondered whether Gunnar's emphasis on Icelandic material—the weather, the wilderness—became more pronounced due to his place of residence; whether Iceland itself, its people and environment, became, in a sense, "greener" or "fonder"—more vivid—in response to distance, as well as, perhaps, because his readers, Danes and then Germans, were enamored of and sought after descriptions of such material. Do these two things, the influence of distance and the thirst of readers for descriptions of the North, explain Gunnar's incredibly long description of the *vikivaki* ring-dance early in his novel *Vikivaki* (1932)? The chapter containing the description is a peculiar bastard. Few Icelandic books begin as originally as *Vikivaki,* yet we can say without hesitation that the novel loses almost all of its unique, peculiar atmosphere after dozens of pages of rustic romance. Why? I can't shake the feeling that with *Vikivaki*, the influence of distance—the strong, even sentimental pull of home—numbed Gunnar's sense of self-critique, to his misfortune. This, in fact, means that I cannot possibly agree with those who consider *Vikivaki* among his best books. The idea behind the novel is certainly brilliant, if not fantastic, yet the same does not apply to its composition, leaving the book considerably inferior to the three jewels, *The Church on the Mountain*, *The Black Cliffs*, and *Advent*.

A man goes to the mountains and is then printed in 250,000 copies

I don't know how many times I've read *Advent,* but for a span of about fifteen years, I read the story of Benedikt and his companions every Christmas, starting on the Feast of St. Þorlákur (December 23) and finishing on Christmas Day, reading slowly, enjoying the experience as much as one might enjoy sitting and chatting with old friends. Various things have been said about *Advent* since it was published, first in German in 1936, a year later in Danish, and finally in Icelandic translation in 1939. No book of Gunnar's has traveled as widely, to more countries than you can count on both hands. It was, for instance, printed in two-hundred-and-fifty thousand copies in the United States, and there is certainly something to the idea that *Advent* was the spark for *The Old Man and the Sea* by Ernest Hemingway.

The genesis of *Advent* has its own special history. On December 10, 1925, a group of men headed to the mountains in the Eastfjords of Iceland to search for sheep. One of the men was named Benedikt Sigurjónsson, nicknamed Mountain-

Bensi, a man with the wilderness in his blood. Six years later, an account of Mountain-Bensi's hazardous journey in the wilderness, written by Þórður Jónsson, appeared in the magazine *Eimreiðin*. In this account, Bensi continues the search for livestock, first horses, then sheep, on his own in the Mývatn Wilderness after his companions head back to human haunts with a flock of sheep on December 13. After enduring great hardships, Mountain-Bensi returns to the farms on the Second Day of Christmas (December 26), to find that folk have begun making preparations to search for him. Gunnar apparently read the story in Denmark, and when the magazine *Julesne* asked him to write a story set in Iceland, he wrote the short story 'The Good Shepherd,' based on Þórður's account of Mountain-Bensi. The short story is 'mainly a poetically stylized retelling of the account of Mountain-Bensi's journey,' wrote the critic Ólafur Jónsson. Five years passed, and then the German publishing house Reclam contacted Gunnar and asked him to write a novella for their series Reclam Universal Bibliothek and *Advent* was born. The story itself, its protagonist, Benedikt, and his search for sheep in the wilderness in the second-most vicious month of the Icelandic winter, thus has its roots in what we call reality, as opposed to fiction, although the distinction between them is more dubious than many believe, so dubious that trying to draw clear lines between the two could directly jeopardize one's mental health. It is of course nice to know the stories behind books, the models for their characters, the events that set fictional accounts in motion, creating worlds parallel to this one; such information is enjoyable, yet is irrelevant, all the same—chaff—because what matters is the world of the book, the literary creation, and books should always be read on their terms, as they stand or fall in and of themselves, not elsewise. Yet for those who wish to acquaint themselves with Gunnar's working methods, reflect on the genesis of books and in doing so attempt to better understand the writer behind the words, it doesn't hurt to compare "The Good Shepherd" and *Advent,* for by doing so, we get an unexpected chance to snoop around in Gunnar's studio, observe him whittling ideas, giving them greater depth, see how he gradually distances himself from events and characters that set everything in motion, distances himself from models and creates his own world. We see how he whittles down a long account in "The Good Shepherd" —half a biography, almost—to three lines in *Advent*; here I mean the description of the relationship between Benedikt and Sigríður of Botn. A dramatic story, turbulent emotions, an account of a shipwreck, and an unusual reconciliation, all of this is written in such a way that it seems almost to hover invisibly in the words; so masterful is Gunnar with the style of *Advent*, at ease and disciplined at once, that he manages to squeeze it all in without us noticing, simply by creating an atmosphere that we sense, that we breathe in—that we live.

A man roams the wilderness with a dog and a ram in December, searching for sheep, gets caught in a storm yet makes it back to human habitations alive; this is the story of *Advent*. Simple on the surface. I wouldn't exactly call what's below the surface complex, yet the book certainly does have depth and fertility. The story itself, in all of its simplicity, is excellent and classic: man facing the elements. To that theme, however, are added the style and the author's reflections, partly motivated by the story, partly not, at once familiar and deeply philosophical, opening up to the reader through simple acts:

> The peasant laughed shortly, and as he went in, pinched out the wick with two fingers. It is a service of love for a light not to leave it devouring itself to no purpose ...

From Blicher to Conrad

Stylistically, *Advent* is something of an adventure tale. Gunnar was a master stylist, as witnessed in his books: at times garrulous, even to an extreme, as in *The Church on the Mountain;* hard and coarse as in *Sonata of the Sea* (*Sonate ved havet*, 1955), yet nowhere as straightforward and downright beautiful as in *Advent*. No man, however, is an island in literature; the same sort of style appears in different authors. I don't know how far back it's possible to trace it—perhaps to the Dane Steen Steensen Blicher, who wrote in the first part of the 19th century, and whom Gunnar greatly admired, among other things translating one of his novels, *Præsten i Vejlbye* (*The Rector of Veilbye*, originally published in 1829). It's a unique style; I don't know whether it can be called Nordic, but it achieves a certain perfection in Knut Hamsun, the matchless wizard who influenced so many different writers. Hemingway dreamed of writing like Hamsun, and his admiration for the Norwegian's style could lend a bit of support to the idea that *Advent* appealed to him so strongly that *Old Man and the Sea* was born. Other authors, however, might be mentioned: Gunnar, of course; Halldór Laxness; the Faeroese William Heinesen, and the Dane Martin A. Hansen. But where does this style come from; why were Nordic authors drawn to it? Is it the combination of weather and light, long, dark winters, and summer nights so bright that they give nothing rest? A dreamy realism, poetic narrative, quiet in nature, yet nevertheless accommodating the scream that Edvard Munch captured on canvas; composure that is a kind of complacency, likely sprung from depression. In this style, darkness does not reign, but neither does light; perhaps it is twilight.

One element that marks *Advent* so strongly, as well as *The Church on the Mountain*, I might add, is Gunnar's description of the weather. I can hardly recall having read —how shall I say it—such strong, convincing descriptions of storms as Gunnar's—except perhaps those of Joseph Conrad. I'm often reminded of Gunnar when reading

Conrad and encountering his descriptions of the fury of storms on the open sea, and likewise, I'm reminded of Conrad when Gunnar starts describing storms in the mountains. Both writers strike such familiar chords in the reader with these descriptions of the raging forces of nature that he cowers instinctively, which is perhaps a natural reaction when confronted with forces over which we have no control; something in the deepest recesses of our memories commands us to cower, make ourselves smaller, revert to tiny mammals huddling in our holes at the approach of something incredibly big: a dinosaur or meteorite. Is there not an affinity between Gunnar and Conrad—and I don't just mean in their unique ability to describe the weather? Gunnar was an Icelander who wrote in Danish, a language that he learned following adolescence; Conrad was a Pole who wrote in English, a language that he also learned following adolescence. Both are known for their grasp of language, surpassing most native authors in that regard; both are philosophical and put a great deal into structuring their narratives—novelists par excellence. Gunnar was undoubtedly familiar with Conrad, most of the Pole's books having been published in Danish translation by the time Gunnar set foot in Denmark—presumably to conquer the world.

On deep-rooted familiarity

Benedikt travels with a dog and a ram; they are his companions. An account of a man who travels alone, page after page, and what's more, without his head full of ancient wisdom, like Aschenbach in *Death in Venice*—wisdom that proves, of course, inadequate against the violence of emotions. This man, Benedikt, who knows little about Greek gods, even less about German philosophers, is certainly caught up in the violence of emotions, like Aschenbach, yet proves victorious—and an author who creates such a character needs to solve various technical problems. For how, if the author does not wish to intrude constantly, is he to fill the pages with words and actions? By what means can he create life and movement around Benedikt, who tramps his way, first up from the farmland, then alone through the wilderness, which can be so antagonistic to all of mankind? Alone? What am I saying? He is so far from being alone—there are three of them, the Holy Trinity! Yet it is one thing to have a dog and ram in one's company, another thing to give them all such clear, personal characteristics as Leó and Eitill have. You generally forget that what you have are a man and two animals, in your mind they are three companions, not a man and animals. Eitill is serious, grave, yet trusty and gritty, while Leó is something of a clown, albeit indispensable when the going gets tough. He is in fact the book's scene-stealer; Gunnar inserts half a sentence in connection with him here and there, simple observations about dogs, yet in a way that makes the reader smile and feel for a moment as if the world is darned amusing. Gunnar actually removes all doubt at the start of the story that the three are first and foremost companions, not a man and two animals, and does it in such a way that the reader fully understands that between the three lies the kind of thread that makes life valuable, the world a place worth inhabiting:

> These three had been inseparable on these expeditions for a number of years now, and they had gradually come to know one another with that deep-seated knowledge perhaps to be found only among animals of such divergent kinds that no shade of their own ego or own blood or own wishes or desires could come between them to confuse or darken it.

This description of the relationship between Benedikt, Leó, and Eitill is also an excellent example of how Gunnar expands the world of the book; simple things are given familiar, I would almost say universal, appeal. We do not simply have a narrative of incidents, events, but also reflections on life itself, on the innermost nature of things. Here is another example: Benedikt has come to Botn on his first day, with the entire trip before him. Botn is situated highest of all farms in the area, with farmland below, and the wilderness itself above. Benedikt is thus at a kind of border, and the following short passage contains not only poetic philosophy, but also a subtle and dramatic description of the essential difference between being down among people and up in the wilderness; here, the reader can sense what awaits Benedikt:

> Queer how human beings walking together
> through darkness are lost to one another. But
> the loneliness of the darkness is different from
> the loneliness of the mountains. After all down
> here it is not so utter; one can hear voices other
> than his own and perceive near-by breathing.
> It is not profound like that forsakenness which
> flows from the emptiness round about and
> the stone deeps beneath, and sends shudders
> through a man clear to the roots of his hair.

Fertility of the reader's mind

Advent has been interpreted in various ways. A review in 1938 stated 'This is a magnificent winter ode,' which 'holds one's attention, despite the thinness of the story itself.' The poet Matthías Johannessen says that a recurring theme in the works of Gunnar was the place of man in existence, to 'be responsible, seek the truth and essence of existence, try to understand man's place, Gunnar Gunnarsson has wrestled with these questions in all of his works...' I must confess that I have occasionally felt that this wrestling match made Gunnar's fiction unnecessarily cumbersome, even hindered him as a creative writer, preventing him from seeking new methods in form, as if he forgot that the search for fiction and the search for truth are one and the same, if not the same arm, then the same body. Or, as someone has written: 'It isn't healthy for an author to think too much; let's leave that to the philosophers.' This, of course, doesn't apply to Gunnar's best works, *The Black Cliffs* being an excellent example —a dark and serious book in which the weighty search for truth sweeps a person along with it, like a dark river.

There is much to the works of Gunnar; they are deep and spring to mind at the unlikeliest of occasions: quotations and characters, even entire books. I recently spoke with a writer who said that he frequently found himself thinking about *Blessed are the Simple* (*Salige er de enfoldige*), which was published in 1920, whenever avian or swine flu came up in conversation, as if that memorable book were a direct description of the pandemic possibly threatening the human race. Gunnar is ambiguous, and *Advent* has likewise been interpreted in various ways. Some have claimed that Gunnar purposefully wove the life and message of Christ into the story—that Benedikt's journey ought to be seen as an allegory of the life and message of Christ. There's no new evidence that Gunnar Gunnarsson ever thought to any great degree about Christ and the Bible; yet *Blessed are the Simple* does take place, for instance, over seven days, which is of course a reference to the Biblical account of creation, and certainly one thinks of Christ and his messages while reading *Advent*. Benedikt is a humble commoner, but it's one thing to be humble, and entirely another to be simple. Some would say that Benedikt has a strong natural and emotional intelligence—he is extremely sensitive to nature and his animals, knows the blades of grass in the summer moors as well as the winter storms up in the wilderness; he is a person who understands innately the core of the message of Christ. Benedikt has the rare capacity to ignore the chaff—he is in fact unaware of it; the core of the message is simply obvious to him. On the other hand, warning bells sound in my mind when Benedikt is described as an imitation of Christ, and *Advent* as a saint's life. I understand very well that some people find it tempting to interpret the novella in this way—Gunnar frequently makes reference, directly or indirectly, to the Bible, which is intimately familiar to Benedikt, being part of his family readings, particularly at this time of year, advent itself; yet it is highly questionable to make these references a principal issue—the main point of the story. A book that gains a reputation for being a modern saint's life, an allegory of the life of Christ, is at risk of going stale in the minds of readers; it is prevented from being interpreted in other ways, and even worse, the book will no longer be read on its own terms, the terms of literary fiction. The reader dresses himself in his Sunday best and reads with the humility of a communicant, but this is how one must never approach literature, whose continued existence depends on the fertility of the reader's mind.

Jón Kalman Stefánsson
translated by Philip Roughton

He went out with the dog and the wether—the whole trinity.

GUNNAR GUNNARSSON

THE GOOD SHEPHERD

The good shepherd giveth his life for the sheep.

John 10:11

I

When a holy season approaches men make ready for it, each after his own manner and kind. There are many ways. Benedikt too had a way all his own; and this was his way: At the beginning of the Christmas season, that is when the weather permitted, if possible on the first Sunday of Advent, he would pack food, changes of socks and several pairs of new leather shoes in a knapsack, and with these a small oil stove with a can of kerosene and a small flask of spirits. Then he would take the way to the mountains, the desolate mountains of Iceland, where at this season of the year nothing was to be found but birds of prey, hard and cruel as winter itself, foxes, and a few scattered sheep, lost and wandering about.

And it was for the sake of these very sheep that he went forth, animals which had not been found at the regular autumn in-gathering. They must not be allowed to perish up there from hunger and cold merely because none would take the trouble or the risk to seek them out and bring them home. They too were living creatures of God and he felt a kind of responsibility for them. His aim then was simple enough—to find them and bring them safe and sound under shelter before the great festival should spread its benediction over the earth, and bring peace and satisfaction in the hearts of men who have done their best.

Benedikt was always alone on this Advent Journey of his—that is, no man went with him. To be sure he had his dog along and his bell-wether. The dog he had at this time was called Leo, and as Benedikt put it, he earned his name, for truly he was a Pope among dogs. The wether was named Gnarly; that was because he was so tough.

These three had been inseparable on these expeditions for a number of years now, and they had gradually come to know one another with that deep-seated knowledge perhaps to be found only among animals of such divergent kinds that no shade of their own ego or own blood or own wishes or desires could come between them to confuse or darken it. There really was a fourth member of the band, the sleek-maned horse, Faxe, but unfortunately, he was too heavy and his feet were too small to wade through the deep light snow of early winter; and besides he was not capable of enduring many days of hard work on the slender rations with which the other three made out. Benedikt and Leo were sorrowful and troubled when they had said farewell to him, even though only for a week. Gnarly took this dispensation of Providence as he took everything else, with the greatest of calm.

So the three of them journeyed through the winter day, Leo in front; in spite of the cold his tongue was hanging comfortably out of the right side of his mouth; Gnarly next in an imperturbable trot; last of all Benedikt, trailing his skis behind him. Down here in this inhabited country the snow was still too light and soft to hold up a man on skis; he had to stamp his way through the snow and sometimes his feet struck against frozen clods and stones—phew! It was a hard matter to make much speed, but aside from this there was no great difficulty. Leo, after the manner of dogs, was interested in everything and in the best of humor. At times he could no longer hold himself in and had to break away; then he would come charging back to Benedikt in wide leaps with the snow spraying about him, leaping up at him, barking, stretching against him, asking to be praised and petted.

"Yes, you are really a Pope," Benedikt would say then.

That was his pet name for his comrade, and from his mouth could come no higher praise.

At present the three were making their way through settled country toward Botn, the last farm before you come to the mountains. They had the whole day before them and were making easy going of it, following the paths from one farm to another, pausing to greet the people and their dogs.

"But at least have a cup of coffee."

"No, thank you, not today."

They wanted to reach their goal early, so instead of

coffee they would take a drink of milk—all three of them. Again and again Benedikt was called on to give his opinion as to the weather prospects. Of course, they only meant ... they would not for anything be importunate or prophesy evil ... but surely there was no harm in asking the question. And someone might add, for instance, "Well, the only thing that I wanted to say was ... I suppose Leo is a dog who can find his way even in the dark and in the whirl of a snowstorm?" They would bring it up as a sort of joke and would take care not to look up, would take care not to call attention even with a glance to the dour and threatening clouds in the heaven. And then they would add quickly, "Of course he can find his way, the big cur."

"All three of us can find our way," Benedikt would answer calmly, and empty the cup of milk. "Many thanks."

"As to that," the peasant would joke, "I would trust Leo the most, except for Gnarly," and then he would disappear for a moment in the house and bring out some tidbit, something for the dog to gnaw on. Benedikt at such times did not say anything about Leo's being a regular Pope, but he merely nodded to the dog to take his time about eating, that they would wait until he was through. Meantime Gnarly would be getting a handful of good, sweet meadow hay. Then they would start on again, the three of them.

Benedikt had not been to church today. He had put it off, had not found time for it. If he expected to arrive at a reasonably sensible hour and rest sufficiently to prepare him for the early morning awakening and the long march of the morrow, then he would have to make full use of this day from the first light on. It was principally on Gnarly's account that he was taking the first day's journey so easily. Let it be understood that Gnarly was thoroughly capable and well deserved the name he bore, but one must be careful and not overdo him at the very first. So that Benedikt really could not take the longer road around by the church. On the first Sunday of Advent this wandering through the tilled land to the edge of the heath was his church-going. Besides, before setting out, he had sat down on the edge of his bed in the farmhands' room and read a passage from the Scripture, the twenty-first chapter of Matthew—Jesus' entry into Jerusalem. But to accompany it he had to imagine the ringing of bells, the singing of hymns in the little sod-roofed church, and the wise, calm exposition of the gospel by the old pastor. And he *could* imagine it too, so well that it was all real to him.

So now he was pushing through the snow—white as far as the eye could reach, gray white under winter skies in the evening, the ice on the lake covered with rime or a light drift of snow. Only the low flat craters rising here and there out of the snow outlined the greater or lesser rings of their funnels in a kind of a warning pattern in all this waste of snow. But what sort of a warning was it they wanted to give? Could anyone ever find out? Perhaps those crater mouths were saying, "Let everything freeze, let stone and water grow stiff, let the air freeze and come down in white flakes like a bridal veil, like a shroud upon the earth, let the breath in your mouth freeze, and the hope in your heart and the blood in your veins grow cold in death. Deep down below the fire still lives." Perhaps that is what they said. And what did they mean by it? Or perhaps they were saying something else. But in any case if you looked away from these black rings everything was white, even the lake in the valley—a glittering white surface, smooth and slick as a parlor floor. For whom? Whom did it invite to the dance?

As though born of all this whiteness, against which only the black crater rings showed, and scattering gray lava pillars towered, ghost-like here and there, there lay a benediction over this Sunday in the mountains that laid hold on the heart; an immeasurable solemnity, white as innocence itself, surrounded the peaceful Sabbath smoke from the low-lying farmhouses scattered far and wide, one from another, almost vanishing in the waste of snow—an inconceivable peace filled with unbelievable promise— Advent—Advent. Yes, Benedikt took the word in his mouth guardedly, that great, quiet, strange, and yet at the same time, intimate word—for Benedikt perhaps the most personal of all words. It is true he did not know precisely what it meant, but there was an expectation in it, a getting ready, that he felt. In the course of years this word had come to contain for him almost the entire meaning of his life. And what was his life? What was the life of men on earth anyhow, except a service, imperfect, never to be finished, upheld, nevertheless, and justified by expectation and preparation?

And then they came to another farmhouse and everyday life met them again with its peasant hospitality.

"At least have a cup of coffee."

"We are, to tell the truth, somewhat pressed for time, the days are so short, so thank you very much."

The farmer took a long careful look at the sky and confessed frankly that he had no great opinion of the weather.

"Well, we just have to take the weather as God sends it," said Benedikt.

The farmer, for his part, only hoped that the storm would not break before night set in. Talk like this was especially displeasing to Benedikt. So then they must be on their way.

"Are they really good for anything, these companions of yours?" asked the farmer. He did not want to let the man go on; perhaps he was seeing him for the last time, who knows? Anyway he had had such a peculiar dream—as real as life: A storm gathering around these three—it would test their very souls, if not worse.

"Isn't Gnarly really a bother to you? Can you depend on him and the dog?"

"Can I depend on him?" answered Benedikt. "All three of us are up to anything."

One should not say things like that in the hour of danger. One should not defy the powers so arrogantly. The farmer stood and watched them go. There they went, the three of them—Benedikt, Leo, and Gnarly; and a man, doubt-filled, deeply moved, dissatisfied with himself, with them, with the world, remained behind them, looked after them, and chewed tobacco. Who in the world could understand people like that—to risk everything, even life? And for what? For a few sheep that belonged to others. For Benedikt had only a very few, and none of his were missing.

It is likely that Benedikt did not understand the cautious peasant either. In any case the three went on their way, rejoicing that today was a good day which no one might spoil—Advent. And as Benedikt's head was so filled with thoughts of the holy significance of this day, and of the Scripture lesson he had read, he got to thinking that this must have been the very day, hundreds of years ago, that Jesus had made his entry into Jerusalem. For he was only a simple man, unlearned in the finer matters of history and theology; good will and devotion often crowded out facts in his mind. And it seemed to him that he could feel in the very air plain traces of that great event, that the day had taken on something of its peculiar sacred character, and had kept it on down through the centuries. Benedikt could see Him plainly before his eyes, going into the great city, splendid in the rays of the sun. He had seen it—its white temple and houses in a picture Bible—and Jesus riding on the ass in the midst of it. The branches that the people cut down from trees and spread out before the feet of the ass looked like frost flowers on a window-pane. But they were not white, he knew that—they were green, full of sap, and something of the sunshine was clinging to their leaves. And suddenly the words of the old Book rang out almost audibly through the air, as though the ether-waves had preserved them, and one need only lend an ear: "Behold thy King cometh unto thee, meek, and sitting upon an ass, and a colt the foal of an ass."

Meek! That was a word Benedikt could understand. He could understand how the Son of God could be meek and riding upon the foal of an ass, for of all things living and dead nothing is too small for service, and there is nothing that is not consecrated through service. Even the Son of God. And only through service. Benedikt felt that he knew that little ass and knew exactly how he felt, and how God's Son felt in that holy hour. He could see plainly before his eyes the people spreading their best clothes on the road. And then he heard some say, "Who is this man?" Really! "Who is this Man?" For they did not recognize the Son of God. And yet they should have known Him, for on that perfect and simple countenance shone a smile, only a little overshadowed for sorrow that they knew Him not. That their eyes were so blind, that the mirrors of their hearts were so tarnished. And at the sight of that troubled smile something, a flash of fire, went through Benedikt's heart.

How blind they must have been! To stand face to face with their Redeemer and not recognize Him. As for him, he was convinced that he would have recognized Him from the first glance. And he would have joined himself unto Him at once and helped Him drive the insolent ones out of the Holy of Holies and overthrow the chairs of the money-changers and the tables of those that sold doves.

At this thought Benedikt pushed back his leather cap and dried his forehead. Walking was no exertion for him now, but these war-like thoughts were driving the sweat from his every pore, for he was a man of peace. Never even in his dreams had he thought of violence against his fellow-men—at least not since he was grown. But the words of the Saviour. "My house shall be called the house of prayer: but ye have made it a den of thieves," awakened burning anger in him.

Just to think—how it would be for the merchant to set up shop and begin his usual cheating in the old sod-covered church. Then there would be an end of all peace. And with these words of Jesus ringing in his ears he felt himself ready for anything that might be required of him—under the leadership of the Master. Money-changers—Oh-ho! Sellers of doves—ha! ha! Sellers of anything—he knew what they were like. Only he would think of them as little as possible. And again he wiped his forehead, for he knew some who bought and sold, the merchant and a few peddlers—of course it was all right to say anything at all about them, but the idea of having to attack them with his fists—well, he was not that kind of man.

So Benedikt had his thoughts, joys, and worries, while all about him the gray day gradually grew dark, the full moon lighted up, a pale torch behind the clouds, and from time to time peeped out fleetingly against the silver sky of evening. Benedikt did not think very much about himself and his journey. Why should he? As the day gradually died, he became, to the eye, only one more vague shadow against the landscape. And yet it was a question whether his conception of himself was not still more formless and confused. He was only a farmhand, a laborer, and had been all his life. Or more precisely half hired man, half tenant. Indeed, there was something halfway, indeterminate about him all the way through. Half good, half bad; half man, half beast of burden. Yes, that was really the way it was. In the summer he worked for wages on the farm where he lived the whole year. In the winter he would take care of the sheep there in return for food and a few clothes. Only a short time in the spring and autumn and then during his wanderings in the mountains before Christmas was he his own master. To be sure he had his own stable and barn for his horse, and he had his sheep and the hay which he mowed on Sundays after church in a rented meadow. So he had a good time of it and he was only a simple man and a servant; and he neither hoped nor strove to become anything greater—not even in heaven. At least no longer. Those days were past—the days and nights when he dreamed dreams and felt yearnings now and then after fortune and freedom. Past—and it was better so, for only in those times had he felt the lack of freedom. Since then he had become more of a man—at least he had become a man. And he hoped that that, too, was not vanity and sinful arrogance.

Well, in any ease he was now an aging man—fifty-four, and now there were no longer very many or very long false paths on which he could lose his way. Fifty-four years—and this was the twenty-seventh time that he had come this way. He knew precisely, for he had kept account from year to year—twenty-seven. When he was twenty-seven he had come the first time, and twenty-seven times he had wandered thus, through the land, to the mountains, usually on Advent Sunday, as today. Ah, yes! time slips away. Twenty-seven years—so deeply buried lay his dreams, those dreams that only God and he himself knew about. And the mountains where he had cried them aloud in his anguish. But at the very first of all his journeys he had left them behind and there they lay safely buried. Or perhaps they were not so safely buried? Could it be that they wandered about in the loneliness of the mountains, like restless spirits that live out their fleeting, perverse lives in the waste of snow and weathered stone? Could it be in reality those same dreams which drove him up there every winter— to see if they had not yet lost the edge of their keenness and had sunk into the earth? But he shook off the thought. No, he was surely not such a pitiful thing as that.

II

And now they had come to the place where they were to spend the night and they were struggling up the rise which led to the farmyard—Benedikt, Gnarly, and Leo. The farm buildings stood on a little elevation with the slopes of the high mountains shutting them in in a sort of half circle.

They were high up—and this was an advantage in the spring because it let the sun strike sooner—and at the same time they were protected. Benedikt drew one deep breath when he had reached his goal for the day, then he turned and looked back down the way he had come. His hand grasped one of Gnarly's horns. How warm it was down at the roots! On his other side stood Leo wagging his tail. And as they stood there a kind of holy peace lay on them. It was not that Benedikt felt the heavens opening above him, but still, there really was a little rift in the sky. He stood not alone on the earth. He felt himself not utterly forsaken.

Not utterly. They stood there and Benedikt looked over the land and drank into his soul what he saw. The cool twilight sank down over the mountain landscape, now that the day was dying, and the pale light of the moon streamed more strongly from a sky along which icy mountains were driving, mountains that seemed as real as the earth mountains with their shadowy outlines growing dim and dull along the horizon. The land seems to be more level on such an evening when the lake is frozen and its smooth surface snowed over. And in the midst of this icy world which seemed to be moving toward dissolution into darkness—he himself a part of the darkling evening—stood the man Benedikt, half farmhand, half tenant, stood there with his dearest friends—his wether, Gnarly, and his dog, Leo—and this world was his world. Here he was a living part of all he could take in, all that he could reach and grasp with his eye and his heart, with his thoughts and his imagination. This world was his and he was a part of this life. Not that he was thinking such thoughts consciously. He was not even clearly aware that the reason he had stopped and was looking out and away was because it was his custom to leave Botn before break of day and he would be high up in the mountains when the gray light would come. He only felt something like an emptiness in his breast—a longing that could not be grasped and explained, a strange, pulling home-sickness. He did not know whether it came because he was to leave the inhabited country for a few days or because this farewell was in itself a kind of warning that sometime it might be forever. Man clings to himself and what is his, over and beyond death itself, and he is afraid to let life out of his hands—life, this most real of all real things, this most pitiful of all pitiful things, the most eternal of all that is eternal. He is afraid of the loneliness on which his being rests, which is his being; he is afraid of not having his fellow-men about him; he is afraid of being forgotten of God. Small comfort it is that; if all goes well, he will be buried here and remain anchored in this earth. And from whatever world lies beyond he hopes, when time allows, to have a view of his home valley. Of course, one could hardly imagine anything else.

And as he stood there, Benedikt could not keep from sniffing with dissatisfaction at a few snow flakes—a few lost, softly falling snow flakes which really had no business here, and which consequently had not before attracted his attention. He was not, indeed, completely satisfied with the weather prospects, if he were compelled to admit it. To be honest about it, one might well expect any sort of weather. He looked up searchingly at the moon. It might be snow—yes, even worse. Gnarly had been so peevish today, and he knew what he was about. Only Leo looked forward to the future with true canine confidence, whirling his tail, and was off on all sorts of visits and adventures, and he asked nothing better. There were moments when Benedikt almost lost patience with his foolishness, but then he would pull his ear in a friendly fashion and say, "You rascal!" And still he could not completely succeed in calming his spirit. He was not satisfied with either the sky or the earth. As he stood here now in the vanishing day, he could no longer put his feelings at rest by fighting his way onward through heavy snow. In the long run the omens of the weather which he carried in his blood could not be lulled to sleep in any such manner. Ought he to have remained at home?

His knapsack suddenly weighed so heavily. He laid it down on the horse block and turned toward the door. But he did not need to knock. As far back as he could remember he had not needed to do this at Botn, at least not on Advent Sunday. The door opened at that very moment and Sigrid, the farmer's wife, came to meet him.

"God's blessing on you," was Benedikt's greeting and his cold, bony hand closed for a moment on her fingers still warm from the house.

"God's welcome to you," answered the farmer's wife, but almost at the same moment she glanced at the driving clouds. Changing her tone, she said, joking, "We were really beginning to hope that you would stay away."

"No," said Benedikt, and after a while, "Well, I have taken off my things, so I suppose you will let me stay overnight?" He meant this for a joke too, but somehow the tone failed to ring true. It was not hearty and it betrayed what it should have concealed. In order to smooth it over, Benedikt, without even being reminded, began to scrape the snow from his shoes. In the meantime, Leo had given the farmer's wife his greeting. No doubt he remembered former visits to Botn, and now he was passing the time of day with the farm dogs. Sigrid stepped up to Gnarly and

"God's blessing on you," was Benedikt's greeting.

scratched him behind the ear. He put up with it, but he did not give the slightest sign. Then she laughed, "Old Gnarly never is really satisfied with things, but I don't remember ever seeing him as cross as he is today."

Benedikt's reply was a mumble. "Is it on account of

the weather?" asked Sigrid, and there was something in her manner not exactly suited to her joking tone. Benedikt did not say much in answer; he stood bent over, scraping away at his shoes. He murmured something of which only the last words were audible, "—for he belongs to the Major Prophets."

"You can almost tell that by looking at him," answered the farmer's wife.

"No, that is not the way I meant it," said Benedikt, coming to Gnarly's defense. "He is a prophet in deed and in truth, and not in his own estimation, in case that is what you meant."

Just then Pjetur, the farmer, came up calmly and deliberately, a little behind his wife, as was always the custom here at Botn on the first day of Advent. Right behind him also appeared his oldest son, Benedikt, and after him a whole flock of children; but they were immediately shooed back into the house, for the night was too cold.

"Into the house all of you, and shut the door. Benedikt will be there right away."

Benedikt spoke to the father and son, looking them full in the eye, while he pressed their hands. He had a way of his own to greet them, for the son was his own special friend, perhaps the only one he had. Nobody knew how he had come to have the name of Benedikt, for it was not to be found in Pjetur's or Sigrid's families, nor was it common in the locality. These two were the only ones in the neighborhood who bore it.

"First of all you will naturally want to get Gnarly under shelter," said the farmer, and stepped up beside the wether in a friendly way. But he was tactful and understood sheep. He was careful not to touch him, even though his fingers itched to do so.

"Let me see. If I remember rightly, he will not touch either food or drink unless you set it before him with your own hand."

"Well, it is not quite so bad as that," said Benedikt, excusing Gnarly. "He is a polite beast aside from his peculiarities. Come on, Gnarly."

Meantime, the housewife had gone about her work. Through the door came an inviting, promising smell of smoked meat, coffee, and pancakes. But the three men were in no hurry. With the wether close behind them, they strolled calmly and comfortably along to one of the outbuildings, to where a guest room was prepared and ready for Gnarly every year. It was a corner divided off from the sheep barn where he had water, a manger and a stall for himself without having to force his way in among his fellow creatures, less important than he by reason of his achievements, and struggle with them for his food, and yet where he had suitable companionship. The water had been placed there earlier, so that the frost was out of it; and now the manger was filled with fresh, sweet hay.

Gnarly sedately plunged his muzzle into the water and quenched his thirst, and then pensively went at the good food. Pjetur looked at him, looked at Benedikt—"So you two think the weather is all right for a trip to the mountains?"

"You will have to ask Gnarly about that," said Benedikt lightly, "I have only human understanding."

"It is not to be despised either if only you make good use of it," said Pjetur, who perhaps had already asked Gnarly and got an answer. Or possibly the question had been only for the sake of politeness. That was all they said. They carefully closed the door, went thoughtfully back to the dwelling through the uncertain moonlight which scarcely deserved to be called light. It was almost a gloom. Cold gusts of wind swooped about them out of the impenetrable night with a strange and threatening suddenness. Queer how human beings walking together through darkness are lost to one another. But the loneliness of the darkness is different from the loneliness of the mountains. After all down here it is not so utter; one can hear voices other than his own and perceive near-by breathing. It is not profound like that forsakenness which flows from the emptiness round about and the stone deeps beneath, and sends shudders through a man clear to the roots of his hair.

A light stood in the house door waiting for them. It had been sitting there for a while, burning for itself alone. A lonely light is almost like a human being, almost as forsaken as a doubting soul; and it changes so strangely as soon as it is not alone, as soon as people come to it. So it was with this light. The three men merely stepped through the door and immediately it was no longer so lonely or forsaken; suddenly it had a task to perform, a duty to fulfill.

Benedikt took up his knapsack that he had laid off before the door, and hung it on a nail inside. A sack of hay, stuffed full, stood ready, leaning against a door jamb. Benedikt smelled of the hay and hefted the sack.

"You must have been thinking more of Gnarly's stomach than of my old back when you filled this one."

The peasant laughed shortly, and as he went in, pinched out the wick with two fingers. It is a service of love for a light not to leave it devouring itself to no purpose, but rather to awaken it again, when the occasion arises, to new life and new service. And besides, it is more economical.

They went into the living room to the woman and the flock of children. There Benedikt, the guest of the house, found his food set out on a folding table under the gable window, smoked meat, fresh from the pot with potatoes in the gravy. A good meal for a cold day—a regular Christmas feast.

"You must think I'm going forth into the desert," said Benedikt, to whom mountains were no desert. For this was the twenty-seventh time, you know, that he had gone into them. He did not say so, did not mention even with a single word that for him this was a Jubilee—a kind of Jubilee

Year—but it came up in his thoughts again and again, like a refrain; twenty-seven times.

"Well, now, once you get away from Botn, it is usually some time before you get another hot meal," said Sigrid, and she kept a careful eye out to fit that he was getting enough, "Eat heartily; Leo is already cared for."

As his name was mentioned, Leo looked up from his corner of the room where he lay coiled up not unlike a snail, a black and white dog with yellow spots, and he waved a friendly greeting with his tail to those great creatures who thought about him and knew how to prize him even when he was asleep. Then he quickly curled up again and went to sleep, making good use of his time.

III

While they still sat there chatting, there came a sudden knock at the door, three times. Guests for the night evidently—although it was a well-known thing throughout the neighborhood that other guests than Benedikt were not entirely welcome at Botn on Advent Sunday. They sat a minute in silence. Then young Benedikt got up.

"It must be the Grimsdal people. They probably figured out that they could keep company with you until they get up to the mountain hut. Their sheep are still out there on the meadows by the glacier river," said Pjetur. Then he went to the door too.

"I am pretty sure it was not only your company they reckoned on. They are certainly expecting you to help gather their sheep—you and Leo and Gnarly," said the farmer's wife. She could not endure for anyone to take advantage of people merely to use their strength and their good nature. Why couldn't they let Benedikt go about his own business alone and in peace? "Promise me one thing—that you will go your own way and see to it that you get your own work done, while you still have food in your sack," she went on, and supplied Benedikt again with meat and potatoes and gravy. That had been cooked especially for him. She would have to see what she could get together for the others.

But no matter how unwilling Benedikt was to refuse anyone anything—especially Sigrid of Botn—he could not promise this, for he knew himself too well for that; so he only went on eating in silence.

"If they get there too late that is their own loss. And if you once start in and waste your time gathering up their sheep, you will surely lose a couple of days."

"Well, now ... lose them?" Benedikt picked up her word. "That depends on how you take it." He would have preferred to be spared the long discussion about the inevitable. For if a man came along who wanted to gather in his sheep and if he and Leo and Gnarly were there and able to help, were even indispensable, what else was there for him to do than to put himself at the man's disposal? To be sure he sighed over this new and unexpected annoyance, but that was the way it was, and it could not be helped.

"It is going to make a big hole in your provisions," Sigrid went on stubbornly. She knew how stern and unyielding he was, when it came to a question of being sensible and sparing himself.

"Oh, I am well provided for," answered Benedikt, untroubled.

"You are an impossible man, and you had just as well know it."

Now the others came in by the entry way, and sure enough, it was Hakon of Grimsdal with his two farmhands. They did not seem exactly surprised to see Benedikt, but they said, "Why, to be sure, this is your time to go into the mountains and hunt out the old Stremba." They might have thought of that beforehand, for it was a holiday, of course, as much as if it had been in the calendar, that is for Botn and the old Stremba, neither of which was supposed to be visited in winter time. Stremba—Tough One. That was what they called the pasture back there in the mountains between the two arms of the glacier. It was inhospitable and for that reason people avoided it.

"I suppose the weather tempted you to start out on this particular day," said Sigrid, a little sarcastically.

"Just listen to Mother Sigrid!" laughed Hakon of Grimsdal. "Tempted us? Well, hardly. Forced us out, forced us. If you are a farmer and have sheep in the mountain pastures late in the fall, you can't be too tender in your feelings and have too much regard for your neighbors. And besides we can help our Benedikt a little tomorrow on his way into the mountains. He has all sorts of things to carry and we are stout fellows, aren't we, boys? Anyway, I am badly mistaken or we are going to get a good wind at our backs as we go up tomorrow, and a stiff one at that."

"That may well be," said Benedikt calmly. "Well, it is better to have any kind of weather for you than against you. Up there in the mountains."

"If you are along and Leo and Gnarly—" Hakon didn't quite say "your trinity" although one could see that he was thinking it—"we will at least have the hope of finding the mountain hut and escaping with our lives," he said, joking. "No matter how it turns out with the sheep."

"You ought to have brought them home at least a week ago," said Benedikt, but without any reproof in his tone. He was merely setting the matter straight.

"Man proposes, God disposes, Bennie, old man," murmured Hakon of Grimsdal. "Ah, yes, man proposes, God disposes."

But Benedikt was not listening. He pricked up his ears. Could he be mistaken? But he was not mistaken. The storm was already sweeping over the frozen roofs, a lashing, howling drive of snow as though a horde of monsters had been let loose in the night outside. Inside a little hut with a thatched roof, in the midst of the black immensity of night, you no longer think about the weather as something dead and lifeless when you hear it raging. Winter then is a formless thing, but alive, full of life even in its raging wrath, and you can tell by listening how it feels its own strength. Yes, yes, Gnarly had known for sure what he was about, only too well. Benedikt stood up suddenly. He was going to sleep now.

The lost sheep in the mountains, now they would surely be snowed in—snowed in under the winter covering before he had found them and brought them home. For there was no use reckoning that they would be sensible enough to flee to the higher ground, where the storms blew keenest, where, nevertheless, lay their last and only hope, when heaven and earth whirled together in wild confusion and the hurricane raged. You could not expect that. Even though they did flee to the heights, they would no doubt freeze. But now he would go to sleep, or at least be alone. A man should not share his worries with others. Each one has enough of his own.

And so they slept in the little living room of the last farmhouse before you come to the high pastures. Outside the storm raged and lashed, and in the world outside many storms raged and many things happened. For this was only a forgotten corner of the world. Here, at least, only the storm raged—so peaceful was it here. Here only moss and lichen on the stones prolonged their meager existence—living tools of the Creator, in the course of thousands of years transforming into soil the stones, the outpourings of the craters; changing the fires of earth into germ and growth, with the dew of midsummer upon them and the hoarfrost of autumn nights. ... It is a good thing for a man to sleep now and then.

But as Hakon of Grimsdal said the next morning:

"If Sunday ends with a blow,
Monday comes on to snow."

Really there was not much else to be said about this Monday. At Botn the children were the only ones to greet it with pleasure, for now Benedikt would have to give up and stay there. And Benedikt, yielding with good grace, spent his day between Gnarly and the children of the house.

He would sit in the midst of the children and whittle animals.

When he was not outside seeing about Gnarly, a task which, in such weather, required considerable preparation and took up a good deal of time, then he would sit in the midst of the children and whittle animals and birds, carve people, put together rigging made of splinters, and build ships with masts and bowsprit and rudder and a jolly-boat on the hatch, and all the while telling fairy tales and stories.

Hakon and his men played cards and once in a while roused their sinking spirits with a glass of brandy, both of which were good and strengthening to the heart, as Hakon maintained. "Really good and strengthening to the heart." For to be sure his heart was a bit worried about the sheep at the glacier river; but only a little worried, for after all fate goes its own path and the Lord takes care of His own; that, now, had been his experience. Meanwhile he would read the newspaper and he was fascinated by it. For in foreign countries not only do the beasts freeze, the devil take me, even people freeze. The world is just that crazy. Bennie would have a hell of a job there! And not only do they freeze but they die like flies from hunger and misery, even in summer while the sun is shining. You might believe it was a lie if it were not set down here in black and white.

"Well, as far as I'm concerned I'll take our Stremba and our own corner of the world ... And many hundreds and thousands of people, more than in all Iceland with its islands and reefs, are out of work out in the big countries and they idle around and have nothing to do. Just why that should be so bad, I can't guess, here where we could enjoy a little of that idleness. That's what you'd like to be—out of work, eh, boys? And don't tell me that these are wild tales, and the newspaper not worth what it costs. Especially when we get it for nothing. But just so you boys won't get in the habit of laziness and idleness, the way it is in foreign countries, shake yourselves. Let's play one more hand. And you still don't want to play, Benedikt? Then we three will play with the fourth man blind."

Three, with the fourth man blind—oh, yes, Benedikt had learned that game in the past twenty-seven years, only not at a card table, and not with bright colored bits of paper in his hand.

And so this day passed.

IV

On Tuesday morning, Benedikt was up early. A powerful, strong wind was still moving, but the weather had cleared up a bit. The snow did not seem to be falling so endless and thick as yesterday. Besides, Benedikt was accustomed to it. He stood outside in the dark morning and turned his cheeks, first one and then the other, still warm from the bed, to the icy wind. No new snow was falling, only the old drifting. Even so it would give a man enough to do. But it was not impossible that the weather might change its mind and let up during the course of the day. It would be well to be on the way to the mountains and get a part of his journey behind him. Hastening in, he wakened the people from Grimsdal. He was going now, if they wanted to go along.

"I don't want to much!" said Hakon, leaping out of bed. He listened to the wind, sniffed it, tasted it. "Not much. Not very damned much!"

But Benedikt only went on getting ready. It was Hakon's problem whether he would go or not. "Will you take the responsibility?" asked the farmer of Grimsdal.

"For Gnarly, Leo, and myself, yes," answered Benedikt.

"Sail without thinking, end up by sinking," said Hakon and, cursing in a low tone, made ready to follow. "But even if you won't take the responsibility for us, I suppose you won't object to the boys' carrying the sack of hay for you? Well now, Pjetur and Sigrid, thank you. It is to be hoped that we come back alive. If we don't, you will only have more trouble with us. Don't forget the cards, boys."

Benedikt took out of his knapsack a little covering which he fastened over Gnarly's back so that the snow would not freeze to his wool and load him down too heavily on the way. The farmer of Grimsdal asked whether Pope Leo was not going to get his vestments for Mass, too. Benedikt let him talk, tied a string to Gnarly's horn and—"Let's go."

Gnarly was not any too eager and did not take the trouble to conceal it. And Hakon made it perfectly clear that he considered Gnarly more intelligent than his master. But just now Benedikt was setting the pace, and off they went.

Then Gnarly, too, became reconciled, once he saw that they were not going to be governed by his whim. As soon as he felt the string on his horns, he struck out and ran like a dog. He took pains to show Benedikt that he had not opposed the start out of fear or ill-nature. Friendly? No, he was not very friendly today. Leo had to be very careful, for when the storm caught him and threw him against Gnarly or in his path, he got a taste of the horns. But Leo did not allow himself either to become angry or be run over; in this as in everything else he was really a Pope; he did not snap at Gnarly a single time, but devoted his entire attention to showing that he wasn't born yesterday. If the others were to get lost in the snow, he would bring them safely home.

The four men, marching along, had the storm and driving snow almost at their backs. Fortunately. For when they reached the heights and the level, rolling plains began, the wind made their going easier. The snow held them up; only Gnarly with his sharp hoofs broke through now and again. The men had brought some hot coffee from Botn in bottles; in the shelter of a block of stone, they halted to drink it. The darkness had gradually ebbed away from the world, while they were struggling up to the top. Now only the thick driving snow veiled the features of the landscape and gave rise to the uncanny feeling that they were marching on and on in the same spot. But they went on unworried. For if you keep setting one foot before the other, and hold to your direction you get on. Here and there they recognized a sandhill, a cliff, a gorge. They were on the right way. The storm began to die and they could make out the outlines of the nearest peaks and the nearest ranges even though they were still dim; for the driving snow and the low-hanging, wooly clouds wiped out all clear sharp outlines. But the earth began to regain its form, to appear in its customary shape.

So now the men with their dogs and the wether marched

through the short day, marched unceasingly, and, as they walked, one night had sunk into the west. Soon a new one would arise out of the east. The day was so short that they spent it wandering through the mountains, almost before they noticed it. It was gone; a new night came down over them—they walked and walked. There was no speaking, almost none at all, the wind was still too sharp. But as they strode on they hummed to themselves. As part of the preparation for this journey they had laid in a supply of verses, of psalms, chorals, and songs to keep time with as they marched. They took turn about at it, as their mood or the conditions of the weather changed, Benedikt had a song of his own:

> "Snow and storm and a road full of stones
> Strengthen the muscles and harden the bones;
> The man who sits by the fire all day
> Is throwing the best of his life away."

A song that he had made up himself, a good one to hum when the wind roared and tore the words from his lips as if to say: "Let's keep it a secret between us." No, there was no danger that anyone would be able to learn it by listening to him. They made rare attempts to understand one another, but they might as well have spared the effort and not bothered about it. Even when they shouted at the top of their voices the wind tore the words to shreds and swept them across the barrens. There they went, flying along, shot full of holes by the bullets of the driven snow. Hakon, who was beginning to feel the cold, offered his brandy, took a swallow himself, and tried to increase the effect by an old charm:

> *"Pour a cask of brandy into my grave,*
> *Trickle it down through the clay and the stones,*
> *For thirst for a sweet and biting drink*
> *Will still be quivering through my bones."*

And now, as we have said, it was night again. Night: The moon peeked through once in a while—peeked through torn shreds of clouds. The wanderers were only shadows in the night and its waste of snow. Did Benedikt really know where they were? The other three relied upon it. They hoped he had not lost his way yet. Deep in their hearts there arose a great confidence in Benedikt, Gnarly, and Leo—the trinity, as they had grown accustomed to calling them speaking among themselves. But after all what else was there that they could really rely on? Oh, well, don't talk; just keep going along.

> *Make haste slowly, take your ease,*
> *You can't say more by talking louder,*
> *Go gently, that's the way to please;*
> *And shooting only wastes your powder.*

And they did make haste slowly, they did take it as easily as they could. After eighteen hours of walking that might well be taken for granted. They railed about powder with its wasted roar and blaze, but they would not have objected to a cannon to shoot them along the last stretch of the road, even though there would be a risk in it.

They finally came to their goal! Suddenly out of the snow and the night a tiny elevation appeared—the gables of a little hut arose out of the snow drifts. It looked blind, dead, and forsaken, as if sunk in its own gloom and despair. The rest of the house was, of course, somewhere under the snow. They had really and truly come upon the mountain hut, had come straight as a string. Sure enough this Benedikt was a master and a wizard from head to foot. At any rate there were not many human failings to be discovered in him, but to make up for it, to be sure, there were two that were entirely inhuman—he didn't gamble and he didn't drink brandy. But where was the door now? For there must be a door.

Benedikt took his stick, the iron point of which was flattened out to make a sort of spade. He quickly shovelled the door free; the hard-packed snow came up in blocks and then was tossed aside. And so they had a house with steps going down and a little passageway.

They went in, lighted a candle, and in a moment had a charcoal fire blazing on the tiny hearth. First of all, Benedikt took care of Gnarly. He went to the spring for water, for the hut had been built over a vein of water that never froze. While Gnarly drank, he took a bunch of hay out of the sack, shook it up; cleaned, as best he could, the ice from Gnarly's hoofs; and then he rubbed them and his legs with tallow— good old Gnarly.

The hut was divided up into two rooms. First you came into a sort of stable and then into a little room with a bunk. It was a regular little castle, almost.

When Benedikt had cared for his wether he went in to the others. Here where loneliness lurked, so to speak, outside the door, he realized, once inside, how good it was after all to be with human beings, even if they were a bit talkative at times. Already it smelled like coffee. Benedikt found a vacant place by the hearth, hung up his wet clothes to dry, and went about combing the lumps of ice out of his hair and beard.

"Well, we got here."

"Yes, you are a jewel, Bennie," Hakon said magnanimously. "And you have saved our lives. You ought to get a medal that you could wear to church, and a big sum of money from some foreign country. You have saved our lives, as I have said. But after all, what is a man without his sheep? A beggar, old man, and nothing more. A man like that cannot conjure up medals and money by his words alone. My sheep, God knows where they are driving around—if they are still driving around at all. Most likely the wind has swept them all in a bunch into the river. Or they are snowed under and smothered to death in the snow. And here we sit, babying ourselves. But to hell with it! Let's make well of the coffee as long as there is any left. A man never knows what the next day is going to look like. And on the other hand it is very seldom that anything happens so bad that you can't think of something worse."

They filled their cups and sat down, the farmer and Benedikt on the edge of the bed, the farmhands on the floor. And now Benedikt got out his food—bread, butter, and meat, and washed it down with scalding hot coffee. That did them good clear to the tips of their fingers, so that as they ate they sang a little mountain song:

> "Ride, ride, ride,
> Dashing along,
> Over the sand … "

Ah, yes, if they had had horses between their thighs they would not be so stiff now. To be sure too they might be sitting out there somewhere in the snow up to their necks. But now they needed sleep more than song. They began yawning before they had sung two verses, and so they lay down and slept.

There they lay, as if they had been flung down, four sleeping men in a tiny hut in the mountains, buried in the snow. Four men wearied to death, whose breathing at every moment changed into snores, died away, and in varying tones set in again, like the storm they had just escaped. The dogs too were snoring, and, yes, even Gnarly the wether was giving out little sleepy sounds.

And in the meanwhile, high over the roof and behind the snow clouds, the signs of heaven marched past, measuring day and night even for this tiny corner of the world and for those creatures sleeping their leaden sleep in the little hut. They brought night to an end right on the moment and brought forth a new day. Now day was here. Time to awaken. And they did awaken. Something called them up; and stiff and lame, they stretched new life into their tired bodies. They felt that they had barely fallen asleep a moment before. But it was already light in the hut. Up, and put the kettle on the fire!

As was to be expected the Grimsdal sheep were hard to find and gather. The fury of the storm had driven part of them away from the meadows on the banks of the glacial stream. The first thing to do was to find them, and when they finally had them—well, the snow was everywhere hard to wade through and the days were short. They are so short at the time of the winter solstice. If they had not had Gnarly to lead the scattered flocks to the little mountain hut—Gnarly who went fiercely at his work until he too stuck in the snow himself and had to be dragged out, and who constantly shared with the other sheep his own strength and courage—what would it have been like?

Hakon admitted it freely and was not sparing in his

Then he stood and looked after the departing ones.

praise of Gnarly. Leo, too, got his due meed. He was so keen in following even old trails and in hunting out where the sheep were hidden. He even smelled them out where they were covered over in hollows and gulches. Couldn't Benedikt make up his mind to sell him? And that was exactly what Benedikt could not do. No, no! One cannot just drag a Pope off to market.

And in the evenings they sat comfortably in the hut and were put out because they could not get Benedikt to join in the fun. Wouldn't he take a hand even now?

"Well, the three of us will play with the fourth man blind."

One day, two days, three days passed away and the storm had laid. The weather was quiet and comparatively mild—as long as it lasted. And finally, on Friday, shortly after noon, the farmer of Grimsdal started home with his sheep, north to where the farmhouses lay. They had found and gathered up the very last one. Benedikt went with them on their journey as far as the ridge of the heath, which then sloped gently down to the river valley. He received his thanks, a three-fold handshake, nods of the head, and a few words called out in farewell. Then he stood and looked after the departing ones, went slowly back to the hut, closed the door behind him, gave the tired wether feed and water, and patted Leo. He stretched out full-length on his back on the empty bed, one hand hanging out on Leo, his friend and comrade. Rest, complete rest—nothing to do but rest, to pull himself together, to be whole, to be one with his own soul again ... Advent ... how long ago was last Sunday?

V

Man can have many ways to live his life. Many talk, others keep silent. Many have to be among their fellow-men in order to feel at their ease; others are not their proper selves until they are quite alone, at least now and again. Benedikt was not ordinarily unsociable, but on this Advent Journey he was used to being without human company. This village gossip day in and day out wearied him unspeakably up here in the mountains. It did not belong here. In other days, to be sure, he had not been so sensitive to it as this time. Well, a man gets old. What had become of the peace and the profound quietness of last Sunday? What of the hopefulness, the confidence? Was it really only five nights ago? Or no, should he not ask was it so much as five nights ago? In that case he should now have been back at home again, if everything had gone according to his plans. Instead of that, here he lay, worn out like his old clothes. Even his soul was in tatters. Ah, yes, time passes and a man is not young any more.

Had he been asleep and dreaming or was that really a knock? Indeed, he must have been asleep, for Leo stood at the door barking like mad. But he had not been dreaming, for the knock came again, three separate blows. Benedikt sprang to his feet and opened the door. It was a young man who lived near by, Jon of Fjall. "Have you seen our colts?"

To be sure, Benedikt had seen hoof prints, especially down below by the river, and in other directions too, but he had not seen the horses themselves. In any case they were not in the immediate neighborhood. Naturally he had not bothered himself any further about them. It had not occurred to him that anyone would still have his colts outside here in such weather.

"Does your master think that you are old and experienced enough to find your way about alone up here at this season of the year, my boy?"

Jon of Fjall was of the opinion that he could do whatever anybody else could do. That might be well enough, thought Benedikt, but after all he was a young man and still inexperienced. And now that they two were here together he had, so to speak, to assume the responsibility for him. If Benedikt should go his way tomorrow morning without bothering about Jon and his colts and should come home a few days later to find Jon had not come back, but had perished in the mountains, what then? And besides he could very well give Gnarly a day of rest.

"We will see about it tomorrow," and by now he had coffee ready for the young man.

"Do you really think that you would have time for us to

look about a little together?" asked Jon, who was too honest to be capable of sly hints and ulterior motives.

"What is time?" answered Benedikt and in one way it made him feel good, and then again it hurt him a bit that the boy had obviously not counted on his help.

Saturday was spent looking for the colts. And then they found them too. Sunday the young man set out on his journey home with a greeting for the people there.

"Well, even if I haven't got anything more done, anybody would have to admit that I haven't wasted the week," said Benedikt, for a few words of excuse seemed to be in order.

And now he must make use of this day and get himself still deeper into the mountains, in there where there was no longer any road or path from valley to valley. But he felt a sort of a deadness in his limbs, and not exactly disposed to any great deeds. It had been a strenuous week, one could not deny, but it was child's play compared with the one to follow after. The thought affected him strangely that by this day in other years he had already been back home—back home! That by this time he had already overcome everything and saved the sheep. He would be sitting in the little church with a heart full of gratitude and holiday spirit—he would hear the pastor's sermon on the widow's mite or the signs of the sun and moon.

Saturday was spent looking for the colts.

"And there shall be signs in the sun, and in the moon, and in the stars; and upon the earth distress of nations, with perplexity; the sea and the waves roaring;

"Men's hearts failing them for fear; and for looking after

those things which are coming on the earth: for the powers of heaven shall be shaken."

Thus said the Scripture.

Well, he too, once upon a time, his heart had failed for fear, and he had been in anguish at the thought of death, and at the thought of life, too, if you wanted to be exact about it. He had been in anguish—but that was long ago and this anguish too lay buried in the mountains. Nowadays all was so peaceful in him and about him. Peaceful and quiet like the mountains.

Thoughtfully he sat there and packed his knapsack. He must try to shake off his weariness and use the day to go deeper and higher into the mountains—at least a part of the way. In the midst of his packing he arose, went out and looked at the weather. Now what was that over there on the other side of the river? Horses and people, sure enough! It must be the mail about to ferry across. But why? There was no one here with the relay of horses. Benedikt hurried in and started water boiling for coffee. But when the postman arrived he would not stop; he had a sled and a man to help pull it.

"The day is short, old man, and the men to relieve us are slow in appearing. They are probably holed up comfortably somewhere. We must get along and find them."

Over there on the other side of the river the man who had accompanied him thus far was already on his way back toward the south. Grimur of Jökull, the ferryman, stood beside Benedikt and with him watched those far-traveling and oddly restless people disappear toward the north and south. Grimur had no objections to a swallow of coffee now that it was already made. One ought not to despise God's gifts.

"You look as though you were settled down here for the rest of your life and were keeping an inn," he joked, "I have been seeing smoke for a week." He threw down a sack of charcoal beside the hearth.

"I thought you might have used up your supply, so I brought that with me. After all, I am the one who ought to keep the fires going here. What are you doing here, anyway?"

Benedikt told him that he was on his regular trip, and how things had gone thus and so and meanwhile the days had come and gone.

"You can't get a great deal done in one day, especially at this season of the year."

"Clever of Hakon," said Grimur, "and of that Fjall fellow."

"Well, yes, but sheep are sheep, and horses are horses," interrupted Benedikt, and there was no argument about that. "One must do the one and not leave the other undone, What sense would it make if I were to find a few scattering, lost beasts and let whole herds be destroyed? The way it is, Hakon finally got his back, but if Leo and I had not been there to help hunt them, especially Leo, of course—no, no, Grimur, and besides you would have done exactly what I did."

"That I wouldn't, in the name of all that's holy."

"Yes, you would. Yes, you would. Besides there is this one good thing about it; now I won't have to hunt over the Stremba, for I have already been there."

"Of course, while you were at it you had to live on your own provisions—I will bet on that," said Grimur, who in a great many respects did not share Benedikt's opinion.

"Well, yes, but I usually take enough provisions along for half a month. That's aplenty, and Hakon knew that. And besides they carried Gnarly's sack of hay all the way from Botn up here."

But Grimur only shook his head, sulkily swigged his coffee from the saucer, and sucked mightily at a piece of rock candy.

"You look pretty well used up, to be perfectly honest about it. And besides what kind of a way is this to treat Gnarly? Many a man has been hauled up for cruelty to animals for less than that, and you had just as well know it. Of course, Gnarly will run until he breaks down and dies, just like some people, and you know that well enough. And aren't you responsible for him? Now we are going to tie the sack of hay here to this post, for Gnarly is as sensible as anybody and can do his own housekeeping. Then we will fix up water and straw for him. So you see a few days by himself won't harm him at all. By this time you have it in your head that you can't get around coming home with me and getting a night's sleep. When you get there you can fill a sack of hay and bring it back to Gnarly. And you won't need to be living on your own supplies. No objections! There has already been enough swearing around here, when you remember that it is the seventh week of winter—and today is the feast of the Immaculate Conception."

To ferry over a glacial river—where you have to pull the boat a good bit up stream and in order to get across, row downstream several times the width of the river—somehow it makes you feel as if you were going into another country, almost another life. It gives you a sort of pang inside you—how will you come back? But Benedikt was too tired to think. Even on the way up to the farmhouse that lay between the hills, protected from the worst of the north wind, he was staggering from weariness, and he almost fell asleep walking. In the farmyard he looked back. But the mountain hut, with all it contained, was gone, vanished behind the hills. Only the northern mountains still stood in their place, but they seemed infinitely far away, so far that they sent a pang through his heart. For that was where he belonged.

He had hardly pulled off his clothes, before he collapsed and went to sleep. And he dreamed—one moment he was up there in the mountains finding sheep, wearing himself out with them, working, working, One moment Leo and Gnarly were with him, and then they were gone again, and he was all alone with the sheep. Part of them were lazy, part too full of life; and a terrible storm boiled about him, and the going was as hard as it could be, the snow soft and bottomless. And near by him, a man walked, invisible—not only because of the weather—a man who was at the same time friendly and sinister. What did he want of him? And behind his dream he knew time was passing, that it would not stop, that it never let itself be detained by any river and never got tired, that it ran on and on, mysterious as a glacial stream. Time strode forth over a sleeping man as over one dead.

VI

All of a sudden, Benedikt lay wide awake in a room full of moonlight. So it was night. He felt completely rested. And all at once he could no longer stay still. He flung out of bed and awakened the young farmhand in the other bed, shaking him gently, then they sat side by side and as quietly as possible dressed by the moonlight. They stole softly downstairs in their sock feet to keep from waking anyone else.

"Shall we make some coffee?" asked the young man, but Benedikt told him to let it go.

"No, wait until you get back," answered Benedikt. "You will be back in an hour. Then you can make you some. Come." They whispered like conspirators, although they were outside by now. Something drove Benedikt on—he could rest no longer.

"Look what a hurry the moon is in! Tonight I feel like running a race with it a little way. Before day comes I can be halfway to the other mountain hut, and I can get there before evening."

"What sort of a mountain hut is it?" asked the young fellow, still only half awake.

"It is a hole I've got away up there," answered Benedikt. A sack of hay was standing all ready in the pantry. The young man tied it on his back. If the family had been awake, no doubt Benedikt could have had more provisions. As it was he must get along as best he could. In moonlight like this one could live on the air. He would make out all right.

"Snow and storm and a road full of stones ... "

They buckled their skis on, and in the moonlight glided over the ice-gray land that stretched in a circle clear over to the mountains. They were like some mysterious lode, a focus which fled, and yet remained and after all was a definite goal. Soon the high land began to slope down to the river. They made quick work of it. Leo was swishing along like an arrow, barking loud for joy.

Then they were over the river. Benedikt helped pull the boat upstream, put the sack on his back, gave the boat a push, wished the lad a safe crossing, called his thanks and greetings to the family.

Then the boat drove diagonally down the river in the half light of the glistening moon so as to strike the other shore in the right place. Benedikt was alone again in his own country. He went up and greeted Gnarly. And out here in the night and loneliness and moonlight there came over him once more that feeling of the Holy Day of Advent. An echo of tones, of the sound of bells preserved in the air, of

Then they were over the river.

memories of the sun and the fragrance of hay, of a hope-
filled summer land—or was it? Perhaps after all it was only
a peculiar kind of inner peace.

Gnarly saluted the other two with a satisfied "Baa-a-a."
He stood up, shook himself, and was ready. He pressed close

to Benedikt as the latter greeted him and examined him to be sure how he had fared. Yes, he even condescended so far as to return Leo's sniffing, when the latter stuck out his muzzle. Flattered and overjoyed, Leo wagged his tail, and as usual could not restrain himself. He gaily kissed his comrade and even put his forepaws on Gnarly's back. And immediately got a taste of the horns; in all friendship, of course, but still a warning. That was all the attention Gnarly paid him, but Leo didn't go near him any more.

Benedikt was thoroughly pleased with his Gnarly and the way he had behaved. He had made sensible use of his sack of hay and had not wasted any of it. Now he got his breakfast, properly shaken up and in a clean manger, then his bucket was taken to the spring, rinsed and filled with fresh water. And then the three in the hut had their breakfast in peace and harmony. For the hour was at hand.

Benedikt put on his knapsack, tranquilly buckled on his skis, and stood the hay sack in a corner by the door. He slung a line about Gnarly's horns, carefully put out the coffee fire with water from the bucket, and took a last look around the hut to see that everything was in its proper place. Then with his comrades he went out and shut the door behind him.

He flung the hay sack over his shoulders, heavy enough it was, too—and in the moonlight, with the wether at the end of the rope and the dog at his heels, struck out for the mountains. It was cold today and no mistake, but the wind was still and the cold lay on the skin like a cold breath, and did not cut through. They took it easy all three.

"Make haste slowly, take your case ..."

There was something comforting about journeying in the moonlight among the mountains. Benedikt looked up at the heavens. The wheel of stars up there had already made a quarter of a revolution since he had put his head out the farmhouse door at Jökull. That is the way time swings by, whether you follow it or not. There is something lovely about traveling along under the stars, keeping in motion with them. He liked to walk here. The snow-covered mountains looked so low, so far, in the moonlight. Now and then streaks of starlight would play on the smooth, black ice, veiled in night. A journey like this is a sort of poem with rhymes and splendid words. In the blood it turned into a poem and, so to speak, you could learn it by heart like a poem. And besides some impulse drove a man back here again and again to see if everything remained unchanged. And it was unchanged—strange and unattainable and at the same time friendly and intimate and indispensable.

So at last a profound peace came over Benedikt. He felt a security welling up out of his heart, spreading further and further to become all-embracing, inevitable, infallible! All meaning, all worth, all good was summed up in the mere certainty that he was walking along here. And here he went!

He felt exactly like a man, who, at the point of drowning, suddenly lifts his head above the water and is saved. The air flowed toward him like spring water; he drew in deep draughts. This was what his life consisted in—this wandering. And now because this had come to be his life he was ready for anything, everything, and could bid everything welcome. He had no more cares. Yes, one! He was not clear in his mind who would make this journey after he was gone. But no doubt someone would come.

For surely it could not be the intention of the Creator to forsake the poor beasts who went astray here and were not found at the autumn in-gathering of the sheep, when he, Benedikt, should no longer be there. Surely that could not be His intention. For even though sheep were only sheep, still they were creatures of flesh and blood, creatures with life and a soul. Gnarly there—would anyone consider him a senseless, soulless being—or Leo or Faxe? Were their innocence, their confidence less than the feeble faith of men? Benedikt shook his head. Whoever the man to come after him, he could wish him nothing better than such comrades as these. With such companions a man is never alone in the world. Many a man had more than he, different, presumably, but who could have better? It would be rank ingratitude to consider that anyone could have had a richer or better lot in life. Ingratitude and stupidity. As if there could be any better creatures on earth than his three friends. There is something holy and inviolable in the relationship between man and beast. Some fine day he would have to stand there and make up his mind: a bullet for one, a knife for the other. That was the price to pay. That the responsibility to be shouldered. A man had to become master not only over their lives, but also over their deaths. To the best of his knowledge and conscience. That was the way life went. It hurt. Only one who had been through it could understand how it hurt. After all, to a certain extent, all animals were sacrificial beasts—but was not all of life a sacrifice? When it was lived in the right manner? Was not this the key to the riddle, that the power of growth is a power within, actually a self-abnegation, and that all life that in its innermost being is not sacrifice is arrogance, the wages whereof is death?

But let that be as it might. After all it was a mystery too profound. The one thing sure was that these three here in the night and moonlight, between the quiet ranges, were driving on toward a goal. They had a goal and they knew what it was, all three of them. No lofty goal, to be sure, but still a goal.

The stars paled out into morning. The outlines of the mountains too became dim, vanished, floating away in the uncertain gray of dawn. Then it was day. There is something about a day, especially about its birth, that sets a man free and yet lays down for him bounds beyond which he may not pass.

And at daybreak the winds awakened. At first there

were only a few scarcely noticeable puffs from different directions, just as if they were only half awake. They blew a spark of life into the snow which lay soft and fluffy on the surface. But soon enough the wind-people seemed to make up their minds which direction they wanted to come from today. They began to drive their sleighs up and down the hills and to pile up the drifts. Then the last outlines vanished and it was no longer easy to distinguish anything at all. One could not make out the ending of the snow-gray land and the beginning of the snow-gray sky. For all unseen the lowering clouds around the horizon had risen and moved upward, so that finally only overhead could one see the last dim remnants of the sky so blue the night before. And yet it came as a sort of surprise, something almost inconceivable, when a new snowstorm, which obviously had taken a good rest, suddenly roared about Benedikt and his comrades. And although they traveled obstinately on almost as if nothing had changed, they plunged into the smother so completely that they could no longer perceive each other or even be conscious of themselves. But they stuck together. They armed themselves against madness in the roaring storm and the lashing snow. For the snow fell so thick that one could scarcely conceive how the storm could ever accomplish what it was doing, how it could break through the tight-woven mesh of flakes and play with them and not be smothered by them. At any rate a man could scarcely breathe for them. Benedikt gulped in air when he was able, holding fast to the little line which somewhere out in the whirling twilight of snow was fastened to Gnarly's horns, and struggled on. Leo had to look after himself—which he did. And so they went staggering on their way, the three of them, foot by foot, swaying this way and that against the wild thrusts of the storm.

Well, they were groping their way through the wild snow welter, that was all that was left for them to do. Meanwhile, the day passed, the day of which nothing was visible, which could be barely realized as a tenuous lightness in the whirling snow. Benedikt steered blindly on in the direction of the hut, as he called it. It was really only a hole in the earth with a trap door, a burrow, a kind of grave. He had dug that hole for himself twenty-seven years ago, almost in the middle of the range which he was in the habit of searching out. He had picked a slight rise for it. On one hand it was not so high that the door, weighted down by stones, would be carried away by the wind, on the other not so low that water could run in from above.

Benedikt was convinced that he had kept approximately in the right direction and was on the way to his den. He only hoped that the storm would stop by dark, since it had begun at daybreak, and toward evening it would be possible to see a little better. Else how could he find his hole? But the storm refused to lay. It was not concerned with Benedikt's wishes and feelings. It was inconceivable how it found the breath to keep up such a bellowing the whole day long, so early in winter at that. But it did find it. The scanty light that the snow whorls ground to pieces between them became finer and finer, and it was finally ground away to nothing at all—to darkness with the faintest suspicion of moonlight behind it, to a snow twilight, to a whirling gloom. And the madness remained unchanged, a moaning and roaring—as of giants raging one against the other, a struggle of unseen powers reaching out into infinity in all directions—an insane, screaming, bellowing night.

A human being out in such a night as that, miles from traveled roads, far from his fellow-creatures in a waste land, among bloodthirsty mountains, alone and utterly dependent on himself, must keep his heart tight shut. No crevice may be left open for the evil spirits of the storm to enter. No crack where hesitation or anxiety or the madness of nature can seep through. For here life and death are tossed on the scales of a balance. Which way will the balance swing? In such a case courage alone can help; only the invincible, inviolate might of a man's soul can avail. A man simply denies danger and rushes to meet it. It is just that simple— simple for a man like Benedikt.

"Snow and storm and a road full of stones ..."

And then in the darkness he ran right into a block of stone and immediately thereafter another. He must watch his skis, they might get broken, he had better take them off.

He could not go on like this any further. When he got them off he took a closer look at the nearest boulder. He felt it over, first with his gloves, then to make perfectly sure, with his bare fingers, almost as one feels of a horse or cow that one wishes to buy. He stood still a while and considered, smelling the wind. Which was north, which was south? Ah, ha! he surely ought to know that stone! Yes, he had traveled in the right direction, that is what he meant. Only he had gone a bit too far.

He did an about-face and tried to keep his directions straight, did keep them for a little while, then suddenly stopped and struck out in a circle right and left. Now was the time for a bit of luck, otherwise with this back and forth business it would be easy to get the directions out of his head and get lost. And all at once in the night and storm a feeling came up in his feet from underneath, or something; perhaps some peculiar feature of the landscape. With the utmost care he took two long, precise steps and drove his stick down into the snow, now here, now there, and all of a sudden there was a hollow sound.

That was the trap door! He had found the hut. He was at home!

Now the shovel got to work. It was no long task to lay bare the door, which was almost horizontal, raise it, creep in with his dog and wether close behind him. The wether and Benedikt slid rather than walked down the dirt steps. Leo welcomed the noise they made at it with a joyous bark:

Bow-wow! It was more than good, it was an immeasurable relief to get the weather off one's body and not to have to be in the midst of it any more. Benedikt sank down on the hay sack a moment, so completely unmanned by weariness that he could see sparks in the dark. That felt good! Even Gnarly expressed his satisfaction with a thoughtful: Baa. But when he began to shake himself, making a miniature snow storm in the hut, Leo whimpered and at once began to do likewise.

But Benedikt was responsible even here and he had to care not only for himself, but also for his friends and comrades. He fished the stump of a tallow candle out of his knapsack and lighted it. A pair of shapeless figures stood before him in the flickering light, so covered with ice and snow that almost the only features recognizable were their mouths, eyes and Gnarly's horns. Benedikt went to work immediately freeing his companions from snow and icicles, as best he could. If he neglected this the wet would make its way clear down to the skin as soon as the place got warm. The labor of the coming day would be hard enough even if they did not have to plunge in with their skins wet and frozen. To be sure Gnarly was protected to a certain extent in the most sensitive places by his mantle. Last of all, Benedikt brushed the snow off himself and combed it out of his beard, hair and eyebrows. Then he lighted the kerosene stove. There is no great art in getting along in the wilderness with a fire and cooking utensils and all modern conveniences. If the matches are wet, you need only stick them under your woolen jacket to dry against your body. An old household remedy. When the stove was burning, Benedikt opened the door upon the unchained night and got a few lumps of snow in. When it melted in the stew pan, he kept adding more, and in the meantime went hither and yon, braced the door, and stopped up the worst cracks and holes against the wind and snow. Now that was done!

And when he had provided Gnarly with hay, and with snow to quench his thirst, he brought out food from his knapsack; and Leo got his share. The meat was frozen and even the bread crunched icily between the teeth. Well, he would soon have coffee. They shared the frozen food like the good friends they were—Leo and he—shared it like brothers. He would just like to see a man, thought Benedikt, who had a more comfortable time of it in his castle, and a safer time amid the distresses of life; and besides all that, there was the prospect within the next few days of saving a few sheep from death by hunger, and so of being useful to his own parish and, as well, to all mankind and to all the universe.

"For you just remember this, Leo, even the Pope in Rome doesn't have any better or finer time of it than you and I, or a clearer conscience." Leo only whirled his tail in a circle and gladly believed everything his master preached to him; all the more because every sentence of the dogma was accompanied by a good bite of food.

And Benedikt sat there like a pasha with a piece of

meat in his hand, and shared it with Leo as fast as he could get it thawed, which was not very fast. They had plenty of butter, more than they needed, so Leo did not have to eat his bread dry. So there they sat ... things could be worse ... and today was Wednesday ... yes, so it was.

Well, he had been away from home a good week and more. It had been nine days since he had left Botn, and seven of them he had been living on his own provisions; and you could tell it by looking at them, too, that could not be denied. Although Benedikt had been stingy and economized to the best of his ability, there were only seven pieces of meat left, and they not over-large; besides some pieces of bread that he could have wished a bit more generous. Still, what all had the Master not done with two loaves and five fishes? He had filled the multitudes. It seemed unbelievable, but in the face of facts like that it was hard for a man to give up hope. And, of course, he only had himself and Leo to feed with his present supply. But miracle or no miracle, he would have to economize. Nowhere in the Law is foresight forbidden. One piece of meat each day, let us say; that was all he could allow himself. But that had a certain advantage; he would not be overloading his stomach and would be all the lighter on his feet.

But what had suddenly got into the light? And what had happened to the stove? Benedikt pumped it up, but that did not help; it seemed to want to go out in spite of everything, it had just taken that stubborn notion. And still, there was plenty of kerosene. What magic and witchcraft were going on in his good old den? Had some evil spirit crept in to devour the light? Then Benedikt sat in total darkness.

It was not a natural darkness. It was a most unnatural darkness, it burned his eyes and laid hold on his throat and strangled him; and yet it was friendly. It lured him to sleep, coaxed him to sink down and close his eyes. After all why did he need that coffee? Why did he need any more light that night? But was this friendliness real? He tried to get his thoughts together, to collect himself, to think. After all, could the storm still be on their trail here? Had the snow stopped every crack up tightly? Was it trying to smother them down here? He would see about that!

Benedikt arose, hard as it was for him to shake off the intoxication of drowsiness. He swayed to the door and threw it open. A dream had begun to spin in his consciousness, so that he expected to see outside the freedom of a starry night. But still the same vicious storm bubbled and poured about him, and threatened to blow his burrow away in a minute. He let the trap door fall to again, but in such a way that it could no longer be completely covered.

As was to be expected the candle and the stove were now willing to live again, ready to take up their activity where they had stopped a moment ago. And now the coffee was ready, and its fragrance filled the hut. Oh! coffee! Benedikt drank it devoutly. When he was through, he put out the light. Now it was night here. The blood rushed through his relaxed limbs, until, its fury spent, it found peace and calm. Sleep came slipping along nearer and nearer, and then it was there and took him in its arms.

Well, there lay Benedikt in his den, with a woolen blanket about his body, the hay sack under his head for a pillow, close pressed to Gnarly, who slept in his own manner and once in a while chewed his cud in peace and content. And Leo cuddled up close to both of them and whined his comfort, in joyous anticipation of rest. There they lay, the three of them, under the earth, humble, insignificant, scarcely recognizable as living beings. Yet they would awaken to deeds of which no other would be capable, which they alone could do, and for which only they were prepared. Were they, then, as insignificant as they looked? Did they not after all belong to some Eternal Scheme of Things and were they not indispensable to the great whole? And over their heads the night wheeled on.

VII

Benedikt slept like a rock. Sunk in fathomless night. And then all at once he was awake, suddenly, as always, wide awake, and he felt completely rested. Now then, to shake out of his cover and out of sleep before weariness, always crouching in ambush, should seize upon him again. He sprang up and opened the trap door. Moonlight! Really and truly moonlight! So it seemed that the world had, to a certain extent, righted itself again. And so he had not overslept— unless perhaps he had slept a whole day through. Even then there was nothing to be done about it.

"Make haste slowly, take your ease ..."

He had saved over a piece of meat from the evening before. He divided it with Leo, as well as all the bread that could be spared. Benedikt washed down his portion with a few cups of coffee. Gnarly was to be allowed to remain in the cave today and get a complete rest, Benedikt decided. He was the most completely done in by the struggle they had been through and there was no sense in wearing him out, unless it was absolutely certain that he would be needed. If matters went as usual, he would have plenty to do before they were safe at home again. So Benedikt provided Gnarly with hay and fresh snow and even melted some for him, so he could have a drink of water right away; then he cleared out an air hole beside the door, Leo looked on with a thoughtful air, tried several times to catch his master's eye, first gave in hesitatingly, then raised one paw, as if he did not know whether to scratch the snow away again, or what. But Benedikt seemed to have his mind made up, and only patted Leo's head. Then it dawned on Leo that he was leaving the knapsack behind too. And so they went into the moonlight, Benedikt and Leo.

Since he had awakened so early and it was so still and clear, Benedikt wanted to search out first the farthest place, a valley by the edge of the glacier. It would take five hours to get there and five hours to get back, even with the best of luck. And then that would be over. He had seldom found anything there, but it was out of the question to go home without making sure. Benedikt gradually got his stride, stamped to the tops of the hills and swooped like a stormwind down the slopes.

"Snow and storm and a road full of stones ..."

But fortune was not as favorable today as the weather. Not a sheep did Benedikt find—at least not a live one. Only in the bottom of the valley below the glacier, already drifted level full, he found a hole in the snow—or rather Leo found it—a hole that a fox had dug. And sure enough it led down to the carcass of a sheep. He had come too late.

With this find, Benedikt's good humor was ruined and it did not return again all day. This was a bad sign, an evil omen. And still and all, this was a kind of Jubilee Year: twenty-seven times—and he himself was twice twenty-seven years old. It was, God knew, a kind of special year, at least for him, and now it had to end like this. But he had had bad luck from the very beginning. And up here things were not the same as they used to be, although there was no especial fault to find as far as the snow and weather were concerned. But the mountains surrounded him with such a sinister, bleak silence. What had he done to them? Could he help it because he had been delayed? Or was it because of his short rest at Jökull? That would be petty, unworthy, he thought. At any rate he felt that he was excusable, he had come back as soon as possible. Well, then, if they wanted to be spiteful and treat him so unkindly that was their affair. From that moment on he would get on without the mountains. When he looked about him he was looking for sheep—only for sheep. And since not one was to be seen, not even a sign of one, he drove on, his teeth clenched, full of rage at the sullen mountains, back to his hut, to Gnarly, to his home and hearth, in his burrow, his den.

But when he had arrived there and crept into the earth

and had shut the trap door, even his food was not right, nor did the coffee taste good; and that night he slept only a little, and that uneasily. It was something like quarreling with an old friend, after a fashion losing the last refuge in a lone world. And if there is anything that poisons one's peace of mind it is this—to go out after live sheep and to find only dead ones.

On the next day, Friday, he went out with the dog and the wether—the whole trinity. The wind came directly out of the north. The snow spread itself out so gently up hill and down dale, as though it had only one thought—to help Benedikt slip easily on and forward. Or it fluttered in ring dances around the blocks of stone and the great boulders, flinging arms about them with a cold elfin grace. Even at that it was not a good day to hunt sheep, for in such weather they sought out sheltered places and immediately their tracks were snowed over. But Benedikt did not worry about that. He must and would search, no matter how hostile the mountains and the weather might be. And his zeal was rewarded. The luck which had deserted him yesterday when it was clear came back to meet him here in the driving snow. Very early in the day he found two sheep, toward evening a third, and on his way home he ran across two others, making five in all. It was like throwing a net out into an invisible sea, this searching in the driving snow, but still the catch was good. For if one knows the peculiarities of the landscape, and the chosen hiding places of the sheep, and besides has a dog who is a regular Pope, one can find sheep even blindfold. So it was and now, after all, the senselessness of things began to make sense. Things were going as they should, and that helped his good nature to get back on its feet.

But they all three had their fill of trouble with the strange mountain wanderers, all three; Benedikt, Gnarly, and Leo. The two pairs stayed together pretty well, but they wanted to have as little as possible to do with any other creatures. Now they would scamper away, one pair east, the other west; the next moment you couldn't move them from the spot. They had to be driven on with shouting and hallooing and the dog's barking, or dragged bodily through the snow. That took strength.

But Gnarly really was a tough and gnarly knot. And here he found his proper task. He joined company with the strange sheep and persuaded them that he, like them, had only the one thought—to escape the dog and man, and he would be their leader—but naturally in the right direction. Often he would get them together and start them going and then Leo and Benedikt would have nothing to do but pant along behind them as best they could. Then again, the strangers would take a wild fancy to strike out in all directions and they would have to be gathered together again. Or Gnarly would stick in a snowdrift so deep that he could not get out alone, and all the rest with him. And then it was up to Benedikt to break a path with his skis and drag Gnarly along by the horns, while Leo watched the rear to see that no member of the band be lost. Sometimes all six of them had to be pulled out one after another. That was hot work!

So this day passed.

Today there could be no question of taking Gnarly along home to the hut. He would have to remain out in the weather and hold the sheep that they had found, seek food for them under the snow, and get them to eat, else they would fall a prey to their whims and scatter. And since it would be so lonely in the den without Gnarly and since they were almost exactly halfway between it and the mountain hut, where the mail carrier on his way south was due to arrive to spend the night, Benedikt decided in favor of the hut. And then he could send word home by the postman's helper, who would take the horses back north. It would be foolish to let the people at home worry about him.

He walked and walked—out of the day into the night; and at last he arrived. But he had made a mistake in his calculations. He found only the post horses at the hut. The driver must have crossed over the river by the ferry the evening before. His helper, who was to go back north, seemed to have gone over with him. But he would have to come back early next morning, or at least some time the next day. Benedikt wanted to wait for him and enjoy a day's rest, although he had only a chunk of frozen meat left in his pocket. Surely the man from his own parish would have a little something to share with him. On Sunday morning then Benedikt could strike for the west—the third Sunday of Advent.

But it did not turn out so—the day of rest was not to be. On Saturday morning long before break of day Benedikt was again on his way into the mountains, going after the sheep that he had found, and the others that he had not found. It was, after all, out of the question to leave Gnarly in the lurch there. But before he left the hut, Benedikt gave the post horses water and hay; so then the helper would be sure to see that he had been there and would be able to figure out from this that he was getting along all right.

In the gray morning dusk of Saturday the wind rose to a storm again. It was a mountain blizzard, a winter storm, a mountain hurricane which shut the lonely wanderer in like a wall. He had to wade through walls, yes, mountains of driving snow. But in some inconceivable way, unknown even to himself, he kept his sense of landscape and direction right, and finally came on Gnarly and the little flock of sheep still holding together. And now they went north again in the teeth of the wind, toward the valley and the farmsteads; slowly, step by step, sometimes scarcely even that, they made their way. Again it fell to Benedikt to wade through the snow drifts and drag out the exhausted, contrary sheep after him. Only Gnarly followed faithfully in his footsteps.

Again it was evening. The struggle with the silly sheep and the insane weather had taken terrible toll of Benedikt's strength. And besides he was beginning to feel the effects of hunger. It had been some time since he had eaten anything, and even before that he had been on half rations. For a while he had almost hoped that he would reach the cave with his sheep before evening set in. But the road and the weather conspired against him. He had to give up, had to leave the sheep one more night in Gnarly's care, and seek his cave alone. So helpless is man. So hard is it to kick against the pricks when the pricks are in the hands of a higher power.

As he calculated there must be about two hours more to go. So he walked, guided only by his instincts, for two more hours. But no hut was to be found, no cave, no burrow, no den to creep into. Oh, well!

There are times when the earth becomes so hostile to man that it closes its doors against him utterly. Then he must look to himself to see what he can do. But still Benedikt found a way. That is the task laid upon man— to find a way, and that is perhaps the only task laid upon him—never to give up, to kick against the pricks no matter how sharp they may be. Even against the prick of death until it forces its way in and strikes the heart. That is the duty of man.

When the feet refuse to do their duty, well, then a man must give up using them, but even that does not mean he must give up. All they want is to rest, that is easy to understand. Let them rest. How good it would feel to rest, just to sit down. And with a troubled heart but with courage unshaken, Benedikt set his stick up in the snow pointing north so that he would know the directions when he got up again. Then he let himself sink down into a snow drift in the shelter of a hill, and with Leo beside him he lay a while and let the snow drift over him, let himself be snowed under. Then he rose on all fours, with his arched back he made a vaulted roof over him, and wallowed from side to side to make a cave in the snow. This should be their house—a kind of house. So they sat in their cave in the snow; and overhead the world roared by.

At first it was comfortably warm here in the little hollow under the snow. Benedikt even permitted himself a nap now and then. But then when his clothes began to thaw out all warmth vanished from his body and he sat there in wet things, his comfort at an end. But he must take a good rest, that was why he was here; and Benedikt rested as best he could, slumbered, and at the same time, took good care not to fall fast asleep. For if he once went sound asleep under the snow, hungry and exhausted as he was, it was very likely that he would never awaken again to this life.

Suddenly he started out of his slumber and he was instantly aware of the fact that he could stay there no longer. So fighting their way up, packing the snow aside, he and Leo broke through two or three yards of it. But where was his alpenstock? It was no longer to be found. The snow had swallowed it up. It was a very enticing idea—that of creeping back into the hole, of remaining under the snow, for the storm was raging worse than before and he estimated that the temperature had fallen to 30° Centigrade below zero instead of the usual 20°. But it was now or never. If he gave up now, it would not mean merely for today, but for all time. Then they would find him here when the snow melted—in case they found him at all. No, the warmth down below, and the refuge from the storm would be bought at too high a price. Now there was only a single hope left— to find his cave, his burrow, his den. If he did not succeed in this, then it would be with him as it had been with so many sheep up there; sheep that no one had found until, next year or the year after, they stumbled onto their whitened bones, somewhere in the desolate sand, blown clean of the slime of life.

As for finding Gnarly and the other sheep, there could be no question of that. Today's task was more sharply limited. Today the thing at stake was his bare life. The cold cut through his wet clothes into his flesh, and the storm threatened to stifle him, for his beard was freezing over his mouth. He got out his knife and sawed it off—there was no other way that he could get rid of this capsule of ice that threatened to close over his mouth and his breathing.

How he found the cave in the earth would be hard to say. Benedikt himself did not know. Really it was Leo who found it. Suddenly, as they wandered, he began to scratch in the snow, and sure enough ... Benedikt got down on all fours, wallowed about in the snow and scratched the door free. So they got down inside and were saved. Benedikt wanted to light his tallow candle at once, and the kerosene stove. But then his matches were wet and would not strike. So he laid them against his naked body under his clothes and sat there and dozed while they dried. He gnawed at the frozen meat, bread and butter, but it was too dry in his mouth and he could scarcely choke it down. So he sat down again and slept. Finally the matches were dry. He made a light and got the stove burning. What coffee is, only he knows who has drunk it in a cave at 30° below in a howling wilderness of storm and rocks. And now he could even dry his clothes.

As he sat and drank his coffee, he took stock of his provisions. Four pieces of meat, plenty of butter and a little sugar; but he was even now drinking the last of his coffee. Nothing could be done about it. And tomorrow was Monday and the next day Christmas Eve.

VIII

Is there more to tell of Benedikt and his twenty-seventh Advent Journey? But we too must not forsake him in his cave, forsaken as he is already by God and man—at least so far as we can judge.

So the tale goes on to tell how he, on the next day, that is on Monday, conceived a hope that enough snow might have banked up in the bed of the glacial stream so that he could glide over it on his skis and be able to reach Jökull— since it was now the day before Christmas Eve. But the glacial river, in spite of the terrific cold and heavy snowfall, was still free of ice and snow.

And we must tell that he tried to go straight down to his own parish so as to be at home at least on Christmas Day. But then it happened that he came across another pair of sheep, and of course it was impossible to desert them, at least not until he had got them under Gnarly's protection. And when he had taken care of this he found that he had used up all his strength for this day so that he was only too glad to get back in his hole in the earth.

And the tale tells that he passed Christmas Eve in

getting Gnarly and his flock a little closer to the valley, and that Benedikt and Leo celebrated Christmas together in the cave. On Christmas Day the weather was calm, but there was a heavy snowfall, which again delayed Benedikt and his sheep. The wind came up toward evening, and they had to spend one more night in the cave; so that the second holiday passed like the first.

But on the evening of this day Benedikt had to give up the struggle, with the last little bit of road unconquered. Old, tired, useless, as he said of himself—he gave it up, left the sheep behind in Gnarly's care, and set out down toward the valley—old, tired, useless.

Late in the evening he reached Botn, and was received as one arisen from the dead. But he paid no attention to the words of welcome. Where was young Benedikt? But young Benedikt was not at home. He had gone over to some of the other farmsteads without saying what he had in mind.

"What I wanted was to ask him to go up there with me when the moon comes out again," said Benedikt.

No, young Benedikt was not at home. But the next morning they heard, at Botn, that he had gathered up a few young men and gone with them into the mountains. And before evening set in he was back again—with the flock of sheep. They had put shoes on Gnarly, had tied leather boots on his hoofs and legs, which were torn and bloody from his constant going ahead and breaking through the hard frozen snow. It was a sight for the eyes of the gods when they met again in the farmyard at Botn, old Benedikt and his Gnarly.

"Thank you, my namesake," said old Benedikt, and that was all that was given him to say.

On this day a few peasants of the parish, who had become anxious about Benedikt and knew nothing about his safe return home, had come together at Botn ready to go to the mountains and search for him—and perhaps also for the young men. Young Benedikt stood there before them, his head held proudly high and his eyes steady and shining.

And then he answered his old namesake: "Let thanks be given where thanks are due," he said.

So then this Advent Journey too was ended, the service was finished, and Benedikt again dwelt among men—for a while.